Mourning Wings

NOUHA JULLIENNE

MOURNING WINGS: A DARK SAPPHIC NOVELLA
NOUHA JULLIENNE

Editing by Alexa at The Fiction Fix
Cover Design by 3crows Author Services
Formatting by Danielle Sarah
Interior Design by Diala at Dialareads
Art Work by Michillart

This book is a work of fiction. All characters, places, incidents, and dialogue were created from the author's imagination. Nothing in this story should be constructed as real. Any similarities between persons living or dead are entirely accidental.

Stay Up-to-Date

If you'd like to support Nouha or keep up with her new projects, scan the QR code to subscribe to her newsletter, join her Facebook reader group, join her street team, etc.!

Trigger Warnings

Graphic violence, assault, death, stalking, mention of parental death, traumatic events, sexually explicit scenes (weapon play, breath play).

Playlist

She's my Religion – Pale Waves
we fell in love in october – girl in red
Yandere – Jazmine Bean
Crush - FLETCHER
FMRN – Lilyisthatyou
Pray – Xana
Gasoline – Halsey
Clothes off – Kehlani, kwn
Skin and Bones – 070 Shake

Princesa: princess

Minha borboleta linda: My pretty butterfly.

Foda-se, princesa: Fuck, princess.

Vem-te para mim: Come for me.

Foste incrível. Mal posso esperar para que sejas minha: You were incredible. I can't wait for you to be mine.

Isto é tudo para mim: Is this all for me.

Eu sou capaz de gostar dessa merda: I might actually like that shit.

Não pares: Don't stop.

Deixa-me tomar conta de ti: Let me take care of you.

To everyone who dreams of being pursued by a masked, masc mommy...
I hope this gives you butterflies.

Mors tua, vita mea.

Your life, my death.

Prologue

VALERIA

12 YEARS OLD

I wrap my sweater tighter around my shoulders as I wander in the crisp autumn air. My breath comes out in small puffs, visible in the cold, the leaves crunching beneath my feet.

The orphanage, which also serves as my school, looms behind me, casting long shadows over the garden. The building is ancient, maybe centuries old. My heart beats a little faster as I glance back at the towering spires that seem to pierce the gray sky.

I walk down the path to the secluded area where I go to quiet my thoughts.

The walls are cold and rough under my fingertips, sending a chill through my hand as I trail them along the stone. The creeping ivy, now a deep red with the season, scratches against my palm. Narrow, arched windows line the sides, their glass panes cloudy and cracked. A tightness forms in my chest, and I remind myself to breathe.

This place has been my home for as long as I can remember.

I lost my parents in a home invasion when I was just a toddler. I don't remember much, just vague images that don't quite fit together. From what I was told, no family members came forward to take me in. Even now, it's hard to make sense of it, knowing that no one came for me—no parent, no relative. It makes me feel as if I was forgotten, like I didn't matter enough to anyone.

That's why I love going to the hidden part of the forest. It's my escape, a place where I can be with myself, away from the other children and the noise of the orphanage.

Out there, I don't have to pretend or worry about being forgotten again. The trees don't judge, and the quiet feels like a comforting embrace. It's the only place where I feel a sense of peace, where I can breathe without the weight of everything pressing down on me.

I continue down the path until I see the opening to my favorite spot.

The wind rustles in my hair, causing strands to temporarily blind me. I brush them from my face as I cross the tight entryway of branches. When I open my eyes, I see her.

Camila. The new girl.

She's different from the other kids—quiet, withdrawn, carrying an air of deep sadness and trauma that most of us understand.

My best friend, Isabel, took it upon herself to be the girl's companion. She appointed herself the unofficial orphanage tour guide, chattering endlessly in her ear as she showed her around. Isabel was determined to break through her shell, to make her smile.

At first, the girl remained distant, barely acknowledging her presence, but Isabel persisted, undeterred by her calm demeanor. She found ways to involve her in games and activities, always by her side, offering a stream of conversation even if the girl never responded.

Slowly, almost imperceptibly, Camila began to thaw. She started to follow Isabel, observing her antics with a faint hint of amusement in her eyes. Though she never uttered a word, her silent presence spoke volumes.

The only thing that seemed to catch her attention were butterflies.

I move quietly through the dense overgrowth. As I get closer, I can see her more clearly, sitting cross-legged on the lush green grass. She's humming softly to herself, the sound almost hypnotic. I pause for a moment, my breath catching in my throat. There's something about Camila that feels...different. Then again, it always has.

I step forward, slower this time, careful not to break the spell. My fingers brush against the rough bark of a tree as I steady myself. She still hasn't noticed me, and I wonder if she can feel my presence, if the hairs on the back of her neck are standing up like mine.

Surrounding her are fluttering butterflies of various colors, dancing around her like confetti caught in a breeze. She watches the delicate creatures with an intensity that borders on admiration.

Intrigued by this enchanting sight, I approach quietly, careful not to startle her or the butterflies.

I catch snippets of soft, whispered words seemingly meant for the butterflies alone. I gasp under my breath; it's the first time I've heard any sound come out of her mouth.

I'm mesmerized by the scene before me. Butterflies, usually so elusive and fleeting, found a companion in Camila. They flit around her, landing briefly on her outstretched fingers or in her hair, as if responding to her unspoken commands. It's as though she possesses a secret language only they understand.

Curiosity getting the better of me, I step closer, close enough to see the strands of her blonde hair catching in the light, close enough to notice the way her shoulders rise and fall with each breath.

A twig snaps under my foot, and she tenses, her humming cutting off abruptly. Her head turns slightly, just enough for me to see the edge of her profile, and I freeze, waiting for her next move.

My heart pounds in my chest, and I swallow hard, my mouth suddenly dry. The forest seems to hold its breath along with me, the sounds of life fading into the background. I take one last step, then another, until I'm standing right behind Camila. I can see the way her hands curl into fists, her knuckles white, but she doesn't turn around.

"Hi."

She doesn't respond.

I settle down beside her, the grass cool against my legs. She glances at me briefly before returning her attention to the butterflies, and I watch in silence.

There's a tranquility in her presence that washes over me.

When she finally speaks, her voice is soft, almost fragile. "Hi."

UNSOLVED

1

Valeria

Present

Music pulses through the walls. I'm wedged in a corner of the living room, clutching a glass and trying to disappear into the wallpaper. The place is packed with people laughing, talking, dancing. It's overwhelming.

This is one of Ebonridge's top Halloween parties, where all the socialites and the best of the best go to see and be seen.

I take a deep breath, the air thick with the smell of alcohol.

Everyone is dressed up for the holiday. I glimpse down at my own outfit: a sequined pink top and matching skirt. Then, I glance over my shoulders at the pink butterfly wings strapped to my back. *At least I'm dressed the part.*

My fingers keep tugging at my costume, trying to smooth out nonexistent wrinkles.

I look around, hoping to see a familiar face, someone I can latch onto for a semblance of comfort. Unfortunately, I don't know anyone here except Isabel, who promptly vanished into the crowd, off to have her own fun, leaving me to navigate this chaos alone.

I convinced her to come to this party in the first place, so I shouldn't be upset that she's enjoying herself.

Despite how much I hate crowds, I love spooky season. There's something magical about this time of year—the crisp air, the eerie decorations, the costumes, the thrill of ghost stories and horror movies.

Even the most mundane settings become enchanting and a bit sinister, allowing people to embrace the macabre.

There's an honesty in the darkness that I find oddly reassuring.

While others might seek comfort in the familiar and bright, I find mine in the shadows and stillness.

My attention is drawn back to the party.

Everyone looks so comfortable, so at ease with each other. There's a group of men in the center of the room, all wearing the same white mask with hollow eyes and eerie, expressionless faces. It's hard to tell if they're supposed to be famous horror characters or some kind of cult. *They must be part of the Whitmores.*

The mystery of their costumes intrigues me, and I can't help but stare a little longer, hoping for a hint that might reveal their identities. The longer I look, though, the more unsettled I feel, but I can't pull my eyes away.

One of the guys catches me staring and turns to look directly at me. My heart skips a beat, and a flush creeps up my neck to my cheeks. His gaze, hidden behind the mask, feels intense and unnerving. I swallow hard, trying to play it cool, but my body betrays me as I shift my weight from one foot to the other and tuck a strand of hair behind my ear.

I take a deep breath, trying to steady myself, but the moment stretches on, my pulse spiking faster. His head tilts slightly, as if he's acknowledging my curiosity, and a chill runs down my spine. I dart away, my heart pounding in my chest.

I weave through the crowd, feeling like an outsider, a ghost haunting the edges of this lively, colorful world. My throat tightens, and I take a sip from my glass, the bitter taste of my drink unappealing.

The music shifts to a new song I don't recognize but everyone else seems to love. I try to smile, to look like I'm having a good time, but it feels forced, unnatural. My cheeks ache from the effort.

Why did I think it was a good idea to come here? *Remember the plan, Valeria*, I remind myself.

A woman dressed as a cheerleader stands beside me, looking almost as uncomfortable as I feel. But her slightly glazed eyes and unsteady stance suggest she has had a bit too much to drink. She seems to be alone, nervously glancing around, as if searching for someone.

"Hi," she says after a moment, her voice shaky. "Nice costume."

"Thanks," I reply, smiling softly. "Yours too."

We make small talk for a few minutes, and she introduces herself as Lisa.

Eyes darting around the room, she leans in closer, her breath warm and smelling strongly of alcohol. "Watch out," she whispers, her words slurred.

My heart skips a beat. "For what?"

Lisa's face pales. "I—I can't say," she stammers, shifting uncomfortably again.

"What's going on?" I press gently. She's starting to freak me out.

Before she can respond, Lisa freezes. Following her gaze, I spot one of the masked men staring directly at us. His hollow eyes seem to bore into me, and my blood runs cold, my body unsettled down to my bones.

Without warning, Lisa sprints away, disappearing into the crowd and leaving me alone. *What the hell was that?*

I take a deep breath, trying to steady my racing heart. The energy here feels different now, tinged with something darker.

I scan the room for Isabel. Where the fuck is she? My anxiety is growing. I need to find her and get out of here.

Then, I remember I can't leave before doing what I came here to do.

At that same moment, I catch a glimpse of my best friend at the top of the stairs, giggling as she's led away by a guy in a sharp suit, wearing the same mask as that group. I gasp under my breath. *Fuck.* I have a bad feeling about this. I want to follow her, to make sure she's okay, but she doesn't seem to be in danger—yet—and I don't want to ruin her night.

A guy stumbles into my path, almost spilling his drink. His eyes are glassy, his smile lopsided. "Hey," he slurs, leaning in closer than I'm comfortable with. "You need a refill? Or maybe a dance?" He seems to be dressed up as Pennywise, but his face makeup is all smudged.

I take a step back, shaking my head. "No, thanks."

He frowns, clearly disappointed, but before he can say anything else, I slip past him.

The hallway is less crowded, and I make my way to the back door, my heart lifting slightly when I spy the night sky through the glass.

But just before I reach the patio, my eye catches on the slightly ajar basement door. *Yes.* This is exactly what I've been looking for. The perfect opportunity to snoop around.

Hesitating for a moment, I glance back at the party and make my decision.

I open the door wider and start descending the stairs. The steps creak under my weight, the air growing cooler as I descend. I gulp down the lump forming in my throat.

When I reach the bottom, it's almost pitch-black and silent, save for a light beaming from the far corner and the distant hum of machinery.

A narrow corridor stretches out before me. My pulse quickens as I walk down, the walls seeming to close in around me.

As I approach the end, the light becomes brighter, almost blinding. I shield my eyes with my hand as I step into a large room. The walls are covered with monitors, each displaying different parts of the gathering above. There are dozens of them, and the sight stops me in my tracks.

I squint, trying to adjust to the sudden brightness.

"Hello?" I call out, my voice echoing in the emptiness.

No response. I step further inside, and a shudder ripples through me when I realize how isolated I am down here.

The images flicker on the screen, showing people partying, but there's something unsettling about watching them from this hidden vantage point. Every few seconds, the snapshots switch, showing different rooms, some empty, but others displaying footage that makes my stomach churn: men and women, in various stages of undress, engaging in intimate acts.

I catch sight of a hallway through the monitor, doors lining both sides, some open, others completely shut. The walls are a deep crimson, covered with intricate, almost hypnotic patterns that twist and turn, adding to the disorienting effect.

My eyes narrow on a specific screen. The camera captures a bedroom where a woman is sitting on the edge of the bed, looking distressed, while a man stands over her, talking animatedly. A wave of nausea surges through me. It's Lisa, the woman I met upstairs.

She dashes out of the room, her movements desperate as she tries to find an exit, but she's moving too slowly, her steps uneven. The man behind her is gaining ground, his strides purposeful and unyielding.

The screen flickers for a second, and I swear under my breath, willing it to stabilize. When it does, my stomach drops.

There's a dark stain spreading across the back of her costume, trickling down from her neck. Blood.

My heart races as I watch her struggle with the doors, her fear palpable even from this distance. I want to shout out to her, to warn her, but my voice catches in my throat. The realization sinks in that something is seriously wrong here, something beyond the eerie atmosphere of Halloween night.

The masked man emerges from behind her. In one hand, he holds a length of rope, and in the other, a large knife. His body language is cold, seemingly devoid of any humanity. *What. The. Fuck. Is. This. Place?*

The image switches.

The other rooms appear to be playrooms filled with an array of sex toys and fixtures, displayed almost like macabre exhibits in a twisted museum. Swings hang from the ceiling, restraints bolted to the walls, shelves lined with various tools, their purposes I can only guess at.

Suddenly, one of the screens catches my eye. It's focused on the same masked men I've been seeing all night. They stand in a circle, their heads bowed slightly, as if they're in silent communication. My stomach twists with unease.

I can't believe what I'm seeing. The invasion of privacy, the hidden surveillance—it's all so wrong. My mind races with questions and a rising sense of panic. I need to get out of here, to find Isabel and tell her what I've found.

As I move to walk away, my gaze lands on another monitor, and my breath catches in my throat. There, in the low light of a room, I see my best friend. She's with the guy she went upstairs with, and they're on a bed, but it doesn't look like she's having fun anymore. She looks scared, her eyes wide and pleading.

"Oh my God!" I gasp. Panic surges through me, and I know I need to get to Isabel, to help her. I can't leave her up there, not like this.

As I turn to leave the basement, something stops me in my tracks.

One of the monitors now shows an image of me standing in this very room. My breath falters as I see myself on the screen.

A door slams shut behind me, and I whirl around, a lump rising in my throat.

Go, Valeria. Run.

I charge forward, bumping into someone. Startled, I look up to see a tall figure standing in my path. I scream, the sound piercing the stillness.

Before my voice can carry far, a hand clamps over my mouth, stifling my cries. My body is turned, and panic surges through me as I struggle, my muffled screams vibrating against the stranger's palm. I can feel their warmth on my back, hear their harsh whisper, but I can't make out the words. My mind races, fear gripping me as I desperately try to pull away, but their hold is too strong.

Then, just as suddenly as they grabbed me, the stranger releases me.

I stumble forward, nearly losing my balance as I face them.

The person is wearing a neck scarf pulled up over their mouth and nose, adorned with the image of a skull. I take in the rest of their appearance—black eyes framed by thick lashes, curly black hair, an eyebrow piercing, and fingers full of rings.

It's a *woman*. I glance closer and notice a delicate butterfly necklace resting against the hollow of her throat. The sight of it sends a jolt through me—a rush of recognition—but the memory remains just out of reach, teasing me with its familiarity.

I feel a wave of unease wash over me, pinned by her intense stare. It's as if she can see right through me, her gaze stripping away all pretenses. I feel exposed, skinned, and it's deeply uncomfortable. Yet, at the same time, there's something almost electric about it, like being lit from the inside.

I feel both emboldened and unnerved by her silence.

Her presence alone is commanding, demanding attention and respect. My throat feels tight, and I struggle to find my voice. Try as I might, no words come out. The air between us is thick, and I can't shake the feeling that she knows exactly what I've just seen.

Her gaze slowly shifts to the monitors behind me, eyes narrowing as they take in the disturbing images. I follow her stare, my own anxiety rising as the reality of the situation sinks in.

"You shouldn't have come here."

A breath catches in my throat.

Her voice cuts through the tension with an unexpected calm. It's soft, velvety, wrapping around me like a warm blanket, and I'm startled by the immediate effect it has on me. The sheer contrast between her earlier aggression and this gentle, almost melodic, cadence makes my heart skip a beat.

I manage to find my voice, though it comes out as little more than a whisper. "I...I need to help my friend," I stammer.

Her eyes flick back to mine, and she gives the slightest nod. It's a gesture that feels both like permission and a command, urging me to go.

With a final, shaky breath, I step around her and make my way back up the stairs, the urgency in my steps renewed. The encounter with the mysterious woman lingers in my mind, her image seared into my thoughts.

As I push through the crowd, searching desperately for my friend, I can't help but wonder who she is and what she knows.

UNSOLVED

2

———

Valeria

I burst through the basement door and re-enter the crowded, noisy party. The laughter and music hit me like a wall as my eyes scan for the stairs that lead to the second floor.

"Excuse me, excuse me," I mutter as I weave between people.

Finally, I spot the staircase and race up, my mind focused on my best friend and the image I saw on the monitor. I reach the landing, breathless and anxious, scanning the hallway for Isabel. *Where is she*?

I remember the layout from the screen and head toward the room where I think I saw her. The door is slightly ajar, and I push it open, my heart in my throat.

"Hey!" I shout, my voice shaking. "Get away from her!"

The guy looks up, startled, as my best friend's eyes meet mine, filled with relief. I rush to her side, my hands trembling as I help her up. "Are you okay?"

She nods, tears brimming in her eyes. "I am now. Thank you."

I glare at the man. "We're leaving," I say firmly, guiding Isabel out of the room and back downstairs.

I take her to what I'm assuming is the bathroom, given the line leading to the door. We skip it, hearing a medley of shouts and grumbles, but I just turn my face and scowl at them.

It's unlike me to bare my teeth at strangers, but my best friend is in shock, and I need to figure out what the fuck is unfolding in this house.

As soon as we're locked in, I plop a still-shaking Isabel on the closed toilet seat.

I rinse an empty cup I find on the counter with soap then fill it with water, handing it to her. She gulps it all in one go.

"Did you know that guy?" I ask once she takes a few calming breaths.

Her eyes are filled with tears, ready to overflow, as she nods. "Yes. He's the one who invited us here," she replies, her voice trembling.

It's the man from Vanguard, Ebonridge's elite men's club, an exclusive establishment tucked away in the heart of the town.

The members are all affluent men of esteemed status. Each member is distinguished not just by their wealth, but by their achievements in business, politics, or the arts. Membership is by invitation only.

And my best friend happens to work there.

I lean against the sink, the cool porcelain grounding me as I try to collect my thoughts. My frustrated eyes meet me in the mirror.

"I asked you to get us an invitation to this party," I begin. I can't quite meet her gaze directly, so I focus on the tiles beneath my feet. "I wanted to snoop around, figure out what's going on with the Whitmores. I should've known it would turn out to be something like this."

I swallow hard, the lump in my throat making it difficult to speak. The guilt gnaws at me, twisting in my stomach. I've never felt so selfish. "I'm so sorry, Isa."

Isabel shifts on her seat and takes a deep breath, her gaze finally softening as she looks at me through the mirror. "It's okay. I decided to come with you. No one forced me. It's not your fault." Her hand reaches out to touch my arm. "I chose to be here because I want to help you find out what happened to Camila. Don't beat yourself up about it. We're in this together."

When Isa mentions Camila, my heart clenches, an ache that never truly goes away. I've been searching for her ever since we were torn apart.

We were just kids back then, but the bond we formed was unbreakable.

Losing her felt like losing a part of myself, a piece of my heart I've been desperately trying to find ever since.

"Thanks, Isa." I take her into my arms and squeeze tight.

Isabel nods. "All I wanted was to go somewhere quiet. That's why he took me upstairs. I'm so stupid. I should've known he'd come onto me."

"Please don't blame yourself. You know how entitled those types of men are. They think everyone owes them something, especially women," I say on a sigh. "I'm just happy I got to you before he did anything else."

"How did you know I was in trouble?" Isabel asks, sniffling into my chest.

"I went to the basement to look around and saw a bunch of screens. There were dozens, showing different rooms at different angles. It was so fucked up." A chill runs down my spine. "There's something sinister about this place, Isa."

"He...he asked me to play a game," she says. The image of Lisa running through the halls flashes in my mind.

"What kind of game?"

"I'm not sure. He said something about hide-and-seek," she mutters.

Suddenly, there's a sharp, insistent pounding on the door,

and Isabel and I jump. *Shit.* I almost forgot there are people out there waiting to use the bathroom. They're most likely wondering what's taking us so long.

If I had any guesses, they probably think we're fooling around.

Just then, I hear a voice through the door. "Hey! If you're gonna stay in there any longer, at least let me in. I'd love to join in on the fun," the guy shouts.

I roll my eyes. *Just as predicted.*

Isabel looks at me with a playful grin, raising her eyebrows. "Should we let him in and pretend we were all over each other while making out?" she teases, any hint of distress disappearing.

I roll my eyes. "Nope!"

Isabel is the only person in this world who cares for me. I don't want anything to affect our friendship.

We've known each other since we were toddlers, having met as orphans in an institution. Isabel was abandoned at the orphanage's doorstep as a baby, left without any explanation or note. She had been there long before I arrived.

She became my closest friend and confidante from the moment we met. We shared a bond forged by our circumstances. We were inseparable, finding strength in each other's company, even after Camila came and left.

My mind inevitably wanders back to that haunting encounter in the basement, how that woman's presence seemed to materialize out of nowhere, tall and slender, like something from a dream. Her gaze, intense and unwavering, pierced through me, leaving me strangely vulnerable yet oddly captivated.

I felt small in front of her, not just physically—her stature towering over mine—but also in the way she held herself, with an aura of confidence that drew me in. There was a thrill in the uncertainty, in not knowing what she was thinking or feeling behind that composed façade.

I had an urge, almost something desperate, to see more of her. It wasn't just about her physical features; it was about unraveling the mystery that seemed to surround her. I wanted to peel back the layers, to bring down the mask she wore so I could glimpse the rest of her face, the emotions hidden beneath.

At that moment, I was entranced. Time seemed to slow as we stood there, two figures in the quiet depths of the basement. The world outside faded away, leaving only her and me, suspended in the moment.

When Isabel and I finally step out of the bathroom, the guy who had shouted at us through the door is standing right in front of it, crossing his arms around his chest.

"About time," he says with a smirk.

I scoff. "I'm sure there are other bathrooms in this gigantic house," I retort, having no patience for his antics. "Now, please move out of the way so we can leave."

He stares us down, but after a few seconds, he steps out of the way. *That's what I thought.*

Looking for the easiest and fastest way out of the house, I see a sliver of space leading to the front door.

I take Isabel's hand and guide her away from the pulsing music and swirling lights of the party. Her fingers tremble slightly against mine, a sign she's still shaken by what happened with that guy.

I glance at her sideways, noting the furrow between her brows, the distant look in her eyes. I hope this doesn't linger.

As we step into the cool night air, I feel her tension ease a fraction, but I know she's far from calm.

As we walk further down the property line, away from the mansion and toward the gates, I sense it before I see it. There's a shift in the air, a subtle change that sets my nerves on edge.

From the corner of my eye, I catch a glimmer of movement—a shadow darting between the trees. My heart skips a beat as I glance over, trying to make sense of what I saw.

Then, like a flash, I see it again: the hint of that distinctive skull mask from the basement. *Is she watching us?* The figure disappears as quickly as it appeared, leaving me questioning if I even saw it at all.

I tighten my grip on Isabel's hand in a silent signal to keep moving, my mind racing with unease. We continue down the path, but the feeling of being watched persists. It's unnerving, like a weight on my shoulders I can't shake off. I can't help but glance back toward the trees, half-expecting to see her again.

And there she is. This time, I stop in my tracks, my eyes locked on the mysterious woman. Isabel halts her steps next to me, confused.

The stranger's gaze is fixed on us. I notice details I hadn't before: her honey-colored skin adorned with intricate tattoos, the uneven dangle of a cross earring—one lobe adorned, the other bare.

She's wearing black cargo pants and a white t-shirt with the sleeves rolled up.

The intensity of her stare sends tingles down my spine, a sensation I can't ignore. It's not just fear—it's something else, something that stirs arousal deep within me. The unknown surrounding her, the danger she seems to embody. It all adds to her allure.

Isabel squeezes my hand, breaking the tension. "Val, what is it?"

I tear my eyes away from the woman. "There's someone watching us."

Her eyes widen in fear. "What do we do?"

I hesitate, torn between curiosity and caution. "Let's keep moving," I finally say, my voice steady despite the uncertainty gnawing at me. Part of me wants to go into the forest and ask her what she wants.

We continue walking, the woman's gaze burning into my back until we round a bend, and she disappears from view. But her presence lingers, and my mind races with questions, suspicions swirling like a storm. Is she part of whatever is happening in that house?

Once we pass the gate, I pull out my phone and call an Uber. The wait feels interminable, every rustle and distant sound putting me even more on edge. Isabel stands close, her eyes scanning the surroundings, as if she too can't shake the feeling of being watched.

We exchange a glance. Tonight has been too strange and unsettling to part ways.

The Uber arrives, and we slide into the back seat, the tension in my bones easing just a fraction as the car pulls away from the mansion.

We're headed to Isabel's place, where I'll be sleeping tonight.

When we first left the orphanage, we shared a small apartment next to the university. It was cramped, but it was ours, a sanctuary where we felt safe. Since graduating and getting jobs at opposite ends of the city, we've had to adjust to living apart for the first time. The transition wasn't easy. The first few months, we spent almost every night together, refusing to be apart.

Now, we do it less often, finding a new rhythm to our separate lives. But after a night like this, there's no way I'm leaving Isabel alone. The memory of that basement, of what happened in the bedroom with that creep, the unsettling presence of the woman in the mask—it's too much to face alone.

We arrive at Isabel's apartment, and she fumbles with her keys. Once inside, the familiar surroundings bring a sense of comfort. I drop my purse by the door and follow Isabel to the living room, where she collapses onto the couch, exhaling a long, shaky breath.

I sit beside her, our shoulders touching, a silent reassurance that we're here together. "You okay?" I ask softly, my eyes searching hers.

She nods, though her expression is still troubled. "I just can't stop thinking about what happened. How much further would he have taken it if you hadn't found us? Who was that woman, and why was she watching us?" she asks, now rambling.

"I don't know," I admit. "But we need to be careful. There's something suspicious going on."

Isabel leans into me, her head resting on my shoulder. "I'm glad you're here."

"I'm not going anywhere," I promise, wrapping my arm around her. "We'll figure this out together, just like we always have."

The night stretches on, and the fear and confusion gradually give way to exhaustion. We move to her bedroom, the familiarity of sharing a space bringing me a small measure of peace.

As we lie there in the dark, I can feel Isabel's breath evening out, her body relaxing next to mine. Too tired to change my clothes, I curl my body around hers, bringing my front flush to her back.

That's when I feel something poking me through my skirt.

I reach into my pocket, and my fingers snag around a chain. When I pull it out, the sight sends a jolt through me.

I narrow my eyes, examining the necklace. It's intricate, delicate, with a small, pink butterfly pendant dangling from it. It's the same one the masked woman was wearing around her neck in the basement. My heart pounds in my chest as I try to make sense of it.

I shake my head, unable to provide any answers as my fingers close around the necklace.

This is hers. But why would she give it to me?

How did she even put it in my pocket without me noticing?

One thing is clear: the chain is a clue, a connection to the masked woman and whatever secrets she holds. I will cherish it, keep it safe until I figure out what it means.

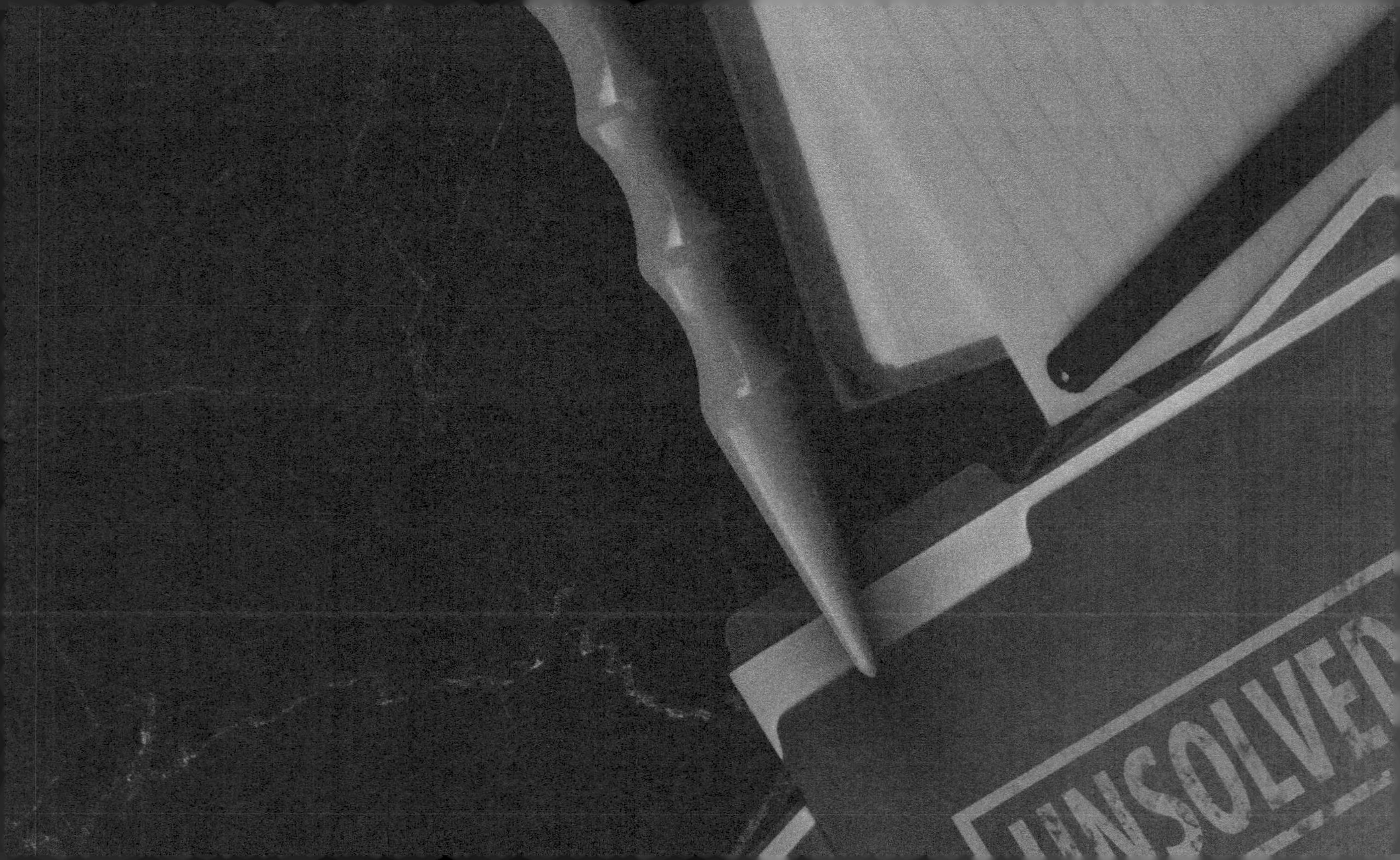

UNSOLVED

3

𝔙𝔞𝔩𝔢𝔯𝔦𝔞

16 YEARS OLD

I clutch the edge of the wooden banister, my knuckles white as I strain to see Camila one last time. My chest tightens, a sharp pain spreading through me as the heavy front doors of the orphanage creak open. I feel like my heart might shatter into a million pieces.

"No!" I cry out, my voice breaking. I try to run after her, but Sister Agnes's firm hands pull me back. Her grip is gentle yet unyielding, and I twist in her hold, tears streaming down my face. "Please, don't let her go!"

Camila turns at the door, her small face pale, eyes wide with the same fear and sadness tearing me apart. She looks so tiny standing there—even though she's a year older than me— her suitcase in hand. The stern-looking couple is distinctly cold. The husband's face is serious, with sharp, angular features and piercing gray eyes that seem to scrutinize everything around him. His wife has perfectly styled blonde hair and a statuesque figure. Her pale blue eyes are icy, her expression perpetually distant, as if she's preoccupied with something more important than what's in front of her.

I want to scream, to tear Camila away from them, but all that comes out is a choked sob. My body trembles, and I feel like I'm falling apart, piece by piece. The cold air in the hallway feels even more biting, cutting through the thin fabric of my dress.

"Valeria, hush now," Sister Agnes murmurs, her voice soft but firm. She pulls me closer, wrapping her arms around me, but it does nothing to stop the flood of tears. I bury my face in her rough, scratchy habit, my hands gripping the coarse fabric as if it could anchor me to something solid.

But nothing feels solid anymore. Camila was the only one who understood me on a deeper level, the only one who knew how to make the endless days in this dark, looming place feel less lonely.

I peek over Sister Agnes's shoulder. Hurt and fear are etched into Camila's expression, the way her hands clench tightly at her sides, as if she's trying to hold herself together. The distance between us feels like a chasm, one we've never had to face before. The words we've said to each other countless times flicker through my mind, and I know she's thinking the same.

"*Mors tua, vita mea*," I mouth silently to her. It's our saying, our bond—an understanding born from watching the delicate, fragile life cycle of butterflies. We always knew one's life often means another's end, but it has never felt as real as it does now.

Her lips tremble, and she swallows hard, fighting back tears. She doesn't say anything, but her eyes speak volumes. There's anger there, but beneath it, I see the raw, aching sadness she can't hide. She raises her hand slightly, as if she wants to reach out, but she stops, letting it fall back to her side, the weight of goodbye too heavy to lift.

I can't bear to look at her anymore.

She nods, just barely, her shoulders slumping, as if the words have drained the last of her strength.

The heavy doors groan shut behind her.

I let out a final, heart-wrenching sob, feeling the weight of it all pressing down on me. My legs buckle, and Sister Agnes holds me up, whispering words I can't hear over the sound of my own broken heart.

4

Ronnie

Present

I step into my office, slipping into the small adjoining room, closing the door behind me. The space is dimly lit, most of the light coming from the array of screens lining the walls. Each monitor displays multiple different camera feeds. The humming sound of my computers instantly offers me comfort, a constant buzz I've grown accustomed to.

I walk to the control panel, its surface cluttered with buttons, plus a joystick for navigating the cameras.

The air is thick with heat, making the room feel like a sauna. I reach for the air conditioning unit mounted on the wall. It's an old model, but it gets the job done.

With a flick of my wrist, I turn it on, and the machine sputters to life, emitting a cool blast that cuts through the warmth. I close my eyes for a moment, savoring the relief as the cool air washes over me.

With my coffee in hand, I sit back on my chair, the screens flickering slightly as I adjust the controls, zooming in on one of the live feeds to get a better look. I'll be stationed here for the next few hours.

For the past several weeks, this has become a ritual for me.

Every day, I open the door, turn on the lights, power up the machines, and watch her.

Across the many monitors, I observe Valeria walking around her apartment.

It's six a.m. As usual, she never misses her alarm. It's almost as if she has been trained to jump out of bed as soon as she hears the first ring.

I was never a morning person until I met her. Met is a strong word, but it's all the same. I feel like I know her from the countless hours spent in front of these screens, memorizing each beat of her breath when she sleeps, every step she takes, the noises she makes.

On more than one occasion, I've caught her in bed touching herself, wearing those slutty pajamas, her taut nipples protruding through the thin fabric. She always looks annoyed when she does, as if she doesn't want to be doing it, as if it's something bad. But as soon as the tips of her fingers reach her center, her body slackens, and she gives in to the feeling.

When she becomes frantic, overcome with sensation, she'll turn onto her stomach to find more friction, more purchase, shoving her blanket between her legs or humping a pillow.

I've watched her bring herself to orgasm on many occasions, the need to jump through the screen and nip at her clit almost unbearable.

Just thinking about it makes me want to spread her juicy thighs open so I can feast on her for breakfast. My center throbs at the thought.

I shake those thoughts away and attempt to focus.

I've been watching Valeria for a few weeks now, but it feels like an eternity.

Every day, I observe her through these screens, learning her routines, her habits, how she interacts with others.

Her days always start the same: wake up, shower, get ready for work, have breakfast, leave. It's so mundane, so one-dimensional.

But I get a kick out of it.

My life is the opposite.

Every waking moment is consumed by a singular purpose: revenge.

I don't remember much of my childhood. It's like trying to grasp smoke—just fragments, distorted images that slip through my fingers whenever I try to piece them together. Sometimes, I have these twisted and vile nightmares that make my skin crawl. I don't know if they really happened to me or if my mind is just playing cruel tricks. All I can clearly recall is being eighteen years old, waking up in a place I didn't recognize, hooked up to machines. I felt like a caged animal, terrified, confused, and completely alone.

I didn't understand what was happening, but I knew I had to get out. So, I ripped the tubes out of my arms and ran. I didn't know where I was going, just that I had to get away.

That's when I met Rachel, the head of the Solace Network. They don't like to call themselves vigilantes, but that's exactly what they are. Since then, I've spent my life helping women like me, by taking down the bad seeds of society one by one. It's not an easy path, but it's the only one I know.

I've dedicated myself to uprooting the predators among us, the terrible people who deserve nothing but death. And the Whitmores are next.

The family has been on my radar for a while now, ever since I first heard whispers about them from my underground contacts. It was always the same story: multiple women dead, their bodies discovered in various places over the years, and somehow, the Whitmore name was always attached. Whether it was near their estate, or the victims had been last seen at one of their extravagant parties, the connection was undeniable.

But despite the glaringly obvious link, they were never once investigated. Not officially, anyway. Call it white privilege or whatever, but the Whitmores always seemed untouchable, never facing the consequences of their actions.

The thought makes my blood boil, and I can feel my jaw clenching as I lean back in my chair. The leather creaks under my weight, a familiar sound that usually brings comfort, but tonight, there's a tightness in my chest that won't ease. I can't shake the feeling that this goes deeper than just a series of unfortunate coincidences.

When I first started digging into the Whitmores, I thought it was just another quest—just another job. But the more I uncovered, the more I felt drawn to them, as if this mission was somehow personal. As if this one hit closer to home than any other before. But why?

My mind drifts for a moment, but I snap my attention back to the screen in front of me.

There's something about Valeria that draws me in, something that makes it hard to look away. I've grown attached to her. It's unconventional, feeling a strange sense of connection to someone who doesn't even know I exist. *Though, she kind of does now...*

Each time I see her, I feel a pull, a magnetic attraction I wish I could resist. I don't understand it.

But I can't afford to be distracted. My focus needs to remain sharp, my mind clear.

Taking a deep breath to steady myself, I zoom in, focusing on Valeria's face, her eyes. Despite her bright exterior, there's something cold and calculating about her, a darkness that matches my own.

I don't know how she's linked to the Whitmores, but every piece of information I gather, every detail I uncover, brings me closer to Valeria. Every moment spent thinking about her is a moment I might miss something important. I'm caught in a struggle between duty and desire.

Valeria stops in front of her long mirror and stares at her reflection.

Her long, honey-blonde hair cascades down her back in soft waves, catching the faint sunlight creeping in through the curtains, making it shimmer against her tanned skin. She's the image of a fucking goddess.

She drops her shorts first, followed by her top, and stands in front of the mirror, her breasts free, nipples pierced, her round ass hugged by her panties.

Fuck.

I settle deeper in my seat and sling my head back to stare at the ceiling. Letting out a huge breath, I squeeze my eyes tight as the constricting feeling in my chest grows.

The attraction is undeniable, but I fight against it, reminding myself of the gravity of my task. I can't let my feelings for her cloud my judgment.

But I can't fucking help it.

When I open my eyes, Valeria reaches up, lightly touching the pendant hanging around her neck, her fingers brushing over the delicate necklace. Her dark brown eyes focus on the reflection, a soft smile spreading across her lips.

It has been three days since I ran into her at the party, and she has been wearing it ever since.

I still don't fully understand why I felt the need to give her that chain, why it seemed so important she have it.

I wore it every day. It's one of the few things I kept from my past, a small reminder of a life that once was.

But seeing Valeria wear it fills me with a sense of contentment.

She finally turns away and steps into the bathroom.

I had the decency to not put cameras in there, despite every ounce of me craving to see her shower.

The thought of invading her privacy in that way is a thin line I'm close to crossing as my mind is filled with images of her under the water.

I imagine the drops glistening down her skin, the way they would trace every curve and contour of her body.

The desire is overwhelming, a fierce pull I struggle to resist.

I want to witness the water sliding down her back, her wet hair clinging to her neck.

I can almost taste it, the urge to lick each one off her skin strong, to savor the sensation of being close to her.

Shaking my head to get rid of the tempting thoughts, I turn away from the monitors and rub my temples. I need to get a grip.

I think back to the night I saw her at the Halloween party.

After watching Valeria and her friend disappear, I turned on my heels and walked deeper into the forest, dead leaves crunching under my boots.

I shivered as the chill penetrated me.

I knew my way around those woods, since I'd been keeping an eye on the Whitmores. Once I caught onto what they'd been up to, I learned the ins and outs of the property.

When I reached my bike, I opened the compartment and pulled out my leather jacket, zipping it all the way up. Out of habit, I reached for my butterfly pendant, wanting to make sure it didn't get caught in the zipper, but it wasn't there.

Right. I had slipped it inside Valeria's pocket when I found her in the basement.

My newest affliction.

I spent hours digging into her background. To my surprise, I didn't find much. She was an orphan who had spent most of her life at Gloomwood Sanctuary until she was of legal age. Then, she went to Ashbury College to study Forensic Psychology while bunking with her best friend, Isabel, who was also an orphan. Now, she lives on the East Side in her own apartment, working as a forensic associate with the Ebonridge Police Department.

But if I was sure of anything that night, it was that she wasn't going home. She'd be sleeping at her friend's house, as she usually did.

If I didn't know any better, I'd think they were a couple, but watching them confirmed the opposite. They're more like sisters.

I hopped onto my bike, bracing each arm on the handles, and lowered my head between my arms. I let a deep breath out. She fucking caught me.

I can't believe I let that happen.

Something about the way she moved, the soft patter of her steps against the cold floor, drew me in.

Her scent hit me first—black coffee and vanilla. It filled the air, wrapping around me, pulling me in. I knew I should have kept my distance, but my curiosity got the better of me.

Step by step, I inched closer, my senses overridden by the need to know more, to see more.

Suddenly, she moved, too quick for me to react. I froze, caught in the act, my heart pounding in my chest. Valeria's eyes met mine, and I knew there was no escape, no plausible explanation for why I was there, lurking in the shadows.

She didn't say a word, her mouth forming a perfect circle. Her cheeks were flushed when she looked up at me, our height difference obvious.

The tension was palpable, like a static charge in the air between us. It was as if our unspoken thoughts hung in the air around us, creating a moment neither of us knew how to break.

I snap back to reality. It was so sloppy of me to have followed Valeria down there, but I couldn't help it. *What was I thinking?* This isn't like me. I'm usually so meticulous, so cautious, but she clouded my judgment.

Before she'd ventured down into the basement, she looked

like a lost deer, standing in the corner alone. I could feel the distress from across the room. It was palpable.

Lonely in a room full of people.

I couldn't stop myself from trailing closely behind as she made her way down the stairs. I tried, but failed, to keep a safe distance behind her. I knew what she'd find down there.

I slipped out of the party but couldn't leave until I caught one last glimpse of Valeria. I knew I should've left, but I was drawn to her.

I wanted her to see me, to feel my presence, to fear me.

I watched as she sensed me before she even fully saw me, her body tensing subtly, and I could picture the way her nipples hardened under my gaze, wishing I could be the goosebumps that erupted all over her skin.

The memory sends a rush through me.

I craved her fiercely. I imagined pulling her into the darkness of the woods, pinning her against a tree, claiming her lips with mine. Instead, I settled for something more subtle yet equally powerful: intimidation.

Her breathing was ragged, her chest rising and falling rapidly. I could sense the thrill in her, even though she looked scared.

Her frightened expression turned me the fuck on.

It wasn't just the fear in her eyes that stirred me; it was the power I felt knowing I provoked such a reaction in her.

Her vulnerability fueled my desire, and I could feel my pulse quicken in response. It was as if she was at my mercy.

Now, as she emerges from the bathroom, I feel a primal need to assert myself, to dominate her in ways that go beyond the physical.

I want to press her further, to see how far I can push her.

As I watch Valeria, a thrill shoots through me.

I'm going to finally make my presence known.

5

Valeria

18 YEARS OLD

The day is finally here, and I'm not sure how to feel.

I stand in front of the small, cracked mirror that's been my only companion in this place, staring at the face that hasn't changed much in the past few years. Maybe a little older, a little sharper. I'm eighteen today.

I'm free.

I grab my old, worn bag from under the bed and start packing what little I have: a few clothes, toiletries, a book I've read a hundred times. It's crazy how little you accumulate when nothing really belongs to you.

The room is silent, save for the soft ticking of the clock on the wall. Isabel is scribbling something in her journal. The other girls are out in the common area, probably waiting for me. I exhale slowly, the breath catching in my chest.

I stand by the door, my hand resting on the worn wooden frame as I look at my best friend. My heart feels heavy, like it's being pulled in two directions.

"I don't want to leave you, Isa," I say, my voice trembling.

"You've been my rock through everything. How can I just walk out of here alone?"

Isabel gives me a small, reassuring smile, but I can see the pain she's trying to hide. "Val, you've been waiting for this moment for so long. You've counted down every day until you could leave and find Camila. You can't put that on hold because of me."

"But you won't turn eighteen for another few months," I argue, more desperate than I intended. "I should stay. We should leave together."

Isabel shakes her head. "No, you need to go now. The sooner you start, the sooner you'll find her. You can't waste any more time. I'll be fine, I promise."

Tears well in my eyes. "It just feels wrong."

She stands up and crosses the room, wrapping her arms around me in a tight hug. "I know, but this is what you need to do. For Camila. For yourself. I'll be right behind you when it's my turn, okay?"

I nod, trying to hold back tears. "Okay."

We pull apart, and I can see the resolve in her eyes. It gives me strength, even though my heart aches at the thought of leaving her behind. I know she's right. I have to go, but it doesn't make it any easier.

"I'll call you," I promise. "Every day."

Isabel laughs. "You better. And Val...be careful out there. You know how dangerous it can be."

I swallow the lump in my throat. "I will."

"Go on, then. I'll join you and the others as soon as I'm done writing."

Before stepping out of the room, there's a soft knock on the door before it creaks open. Sister Maria pokes her head in, her kind eyes crinkling at the corners as she smiles. "Valeria, dear, we have a little something for you in the common room."

I force a smile. "I'll be there in a minute," I reply. She nods and closes the door behind her.

The idea of sitting through some awkward, half-hearted celebration makes my stomach twist. They make such a fuss about celebrating our eighteenth birthday, like it's a new era, like we're being reborn. The irony isn't lost on me.

I close my eyes and take a deep breath, steadying myself. I don't want to be ungrateful. The sisters here have been kind, in their own way, especially given that no one adopted me. I don't know whether to feel disappointed or relieved, honestly. I've lived here for what feels like a lifetime—years of mundane, monotonous existence, just counting down the days until I could finally leave. The thought of freedom always kept me going, a distant light at the end of this long, dark tunnel. Though, now that it's here, I'm not sure what to do with it.

As I head toward the common area, I can't help but think of Camila. It's funny—I used to see butterflies all the time. They'd flutter around the garden in the summer like little pieces of the sun. But since she left, it's as if the butterflies disappeared too.

Butterflies are supposed to symbolize rebirth. But what happens when they're gone?

I dispel those thoughts when I enter the room, decorated with streamers and balloons, all in shades of pink and purple. A small cake sits on the table, the frosting a bright, cheerful yellow. The other girls are gathered around, smiling and chatting, but their eyes keep flicking to me. Sister Maria hands me a small box wrapped in plain paper, her smile a little too hopeful.

"Happy Birthday, Valeria," she says, pressing the gift into my hands.

"Thank you," I say softly, trying to sound sincere. I peel back the wrapper, revealing a small, delicate butterfly pin. I swallow hard, my throat tightening as I trace the shape with my fingers.

"It's beautiful." It's the first gift I've ever received that feels like it means something—but it's also a reminder of everything I've lost.

We eat cake, and I force myself to participate, to smile and laugh. The frosting is too sweet, so I push the plate away after a few bites. The Sisters chatter on about the future, about how this is the start of a new life, a new chapter, but all I can think about is getting out of here, of leaving Gloomwood behind and never looking back.

Once the celebration is over, I grab my bag and sling it over my shoulder. Everyone gathers at the front door to see me off with hugs and well wishes. I nod and smile, feeling like I'm playing a part in a play I didn't want to be cast in.

"Take care of yourself, Valeria," Isabel says, her arms wrapping around me.

"I will," I say, squeezing her back. I give her one last smile before I step out into the cool afternoon air.

The gate clicks shut behind me, and I feel a mix of emotions—relief, fear, anticipation. I stand there for a moment, glimpsing at the world beyond the orphanage walls. It's strange how the sky seems a little brighter, the air a little fresher.

I take a deep breath, adjusting the strap of my bag, and start walking. I don't look back, not once. I have a new life to find, and with it, Camila. She's out there somewhere, and now that I'm free, I'll find her.

And maybe, just maybe, I'll find the butterflies again too.

A FEW MONTHS LATER

I hear a knock on the door, a soft but eager rhythm that could only belong to Isabel. My heart races as I rush to open it —and there stands my best friend on the other side of the threshold.

"Valeria," she says, stepping into my small apartment. The space already feels different with her in it, warmer somehow, despite its cramped quarters.

Isabel looks around, taking in the tiny living room that doubles as a kitchen, the lone mattress on the floor that serves as my bed. It's not much, but it's all I've got, and now, it's ours. I can see the questions in her eyes, the unspoken concerns about how we're going to make this work.

"I can't believe I'm finally here," she murmurs.

Isabel and I haven't seen each other in seven months. We kept in touch as best as we could, but it wasn't the same. Isabel was stuck at the orphanage, waiting for the day she'd turn eighteen so she could join me. And I was here, in this small apartment, trying to figure out how to survive.

On her birthday, Isabel packed up what little she had and made her way to Ebonridge. That was two days ago.

I squeeze her hand. "We'll figure it out, like we always do."

After Isabel settles in, we decide to treat ourselves to some takeout—our first meal together in months. Sitting on the two bean bags that create our makeshift couch in the tiny living room, I finally tell her everything about my search for Camila.

After weeks of digging through every corner of the internet, I finally got in touch with someone who might have answers. Isabel's eyes widen when I mention that I had to go into the dark web to find them.

"Valeria, are you serious?" Isabel's shock is palpable.

I nod. "I didn't have a choice. I needed to dig deeper to get more information. Plus, the guy I spoke to was in an anonymous forum about mysterious disappearances of women in Ebonridge."

I tell her about the guy's cryptic message, how he mentioned a wealthy family named the Whitmores. He described them as predators who look for young women, pretending to be saviors. He wouldn't say much more, only that he could connect me with someone who might help.

Days passed before I heard from anyone, and during that time, I started looking into the Whitmores. As soon as I saw their photo in an article, I recognized them—they were the couple who took Camila away. They're older now, but they still have that same allure.

Isabel listens intently, her brow furrowed as I describe what I found.

"Yesterday, I got a message from someone named Rachel. She said she was part of a group that helps women, and when I brought up the Whitmores, she nearly flipped. They've been investigating the family because of a series of murders around their estate. That's when I started thinking—maybe Camila's disappearance wasn't just a disappearance. Maybe it was a murder."

Isabel gasps. "Do you really think they killed her?"

I shrug. "Who knows. But if one thing's clear, Ebonridge isn't what it seems. It has its problems, sure, nothing out of the ordinary, but there's something darker here. Everyone has a secret, and the more you dig, the more you realize how twisted it all really is."

My best friend shudders at my words. "So, what did Rachel say?"

"I gave her all the information I had on Camila, hoping she could help, but—" Just as I'm explaining this to Isabel, my phone buzzes. *Speak of the devil.* It's a message from Rachel. My heart pounds as I read it out loud.

"Camila was adopted by the Whitmores," I say, my voice shaking. "But she disappeared right before she turned nineteen. They pronounced her dead after they supposedly found her body on the property, but there's no trace of her death anywhere. The Whitmores concealed everything—they even had her body cremated. No autopsy. They didn't even suggest foul play."

The world tilts beneath my feet, and I'm free-falling. I can't get a full breath in no matter how hard I try. Camila...*dead*? My brain can't wrap around the words. It's as if they're not real, as if this is some cruel joke that will unravel at any moment. My fingers tremble as I reread Rachel's message, the words blurring in front of my eyes.

My hands are shaking so much, I can barely control them. My pulse roars in my ears. *She's gone.* Camila's gone. I press my hand to my mouth, feeling bile rise in my throat.

"No," I whisper.

I clutch at my chest, as if I can stop the ache, but it doesn't work.

I feel a hand on my back, and I flinch at first. Then, I hear Isabel's voice, "Val, I'm so sorry."

My breath hitches as a sob escapes my throat. I squeeze my eyes shut, pressing the heels of my hands into them, but it doesn't stop the flood.

I can't even respond; the tears are coming too hard. My entire body trembles, and I feel Isabel sit next to me, wrapping an arm around my shoulders. She pulls me in close, and I collapse into her, burying my face in her shirt.

"It doesn't make any sense," I choke out.

"I know," Isabel agrees. "Something's off."

I sniff and wipe my face with the back of my hand.

"I'm going to find out what really happened. I'm going to investigate it myself." My hands clutch the phone tighter, as if somehow that will keep the last few pieces of my world together.

Isabel doesn't hesitate. "I'm with you, Val. Whatever it takes."

UNSOLVED

6

Earth to Valeria," Detective Nathaniel Bennett says as we wait in line for our drinks at the coffee shop.

I barely slept last night. I've barely slept for the past three nights.

Ever since the Halloween party, my mind's been a tangled mess, caught up in two things that just won't let me rest: the screens I discovered in the basement and *her*, the mysterious woman whose chain is wrapped around my neck.

Every time I close my eyes, her gaze pierces through the darkness, making me feel things I can't quite describe. There's something about the way she looked at me that stirs something deep in my gut.

I've always tried to understand people, to get inside their heads and uncover the truth. I can't ignore the possibility that she might be involved with what I saw on those monitors.

Each time I replay our encounter in my mind, I analyze every gesture, looking for clues, but she didn't give me much to go on.

She was so guarded and barely spoke a word, leaving me nothing to work with but her silence. It was like trying to solve a puzzle with half the pieces missing. She was a mask of calm, giving nothing away, but her gaze was telling a different story. It was intense.

I need to understand her, to figure out what those eyes were trying to tell me. There's a connection between her and the screens, I just know it.

"Valeria?"

Nathaniel's voice jolts me back to the present. I blink, suddenly aware of my surroundings again. I'm in the coffee shop, and my colleague is standing in front of me, holding out my to-go cup and a danish.

"You okay? I've been calling your name for a minute now."

"Oh," I stammer, feeling a rush of heat to my cheeks. "Sorry, I was lost in thought."

"Must be some pretty deep thoughts," he says, handing me the goods. "Here, this might help," he says with a gentle smile.

I take the cup, and the warmth of the drink seeps into my hands, grounding me. "Thanks, Nate," I mumble, trying to shake off the lingering fog in my mind.

He studies me for a moment, concern flickering in his eyes. "You sure you're okay? You look like you haven't slept in days."

I force a smile. "I'm fine, really. Just a lot on my mind."

"Well, if you need to talk, I'm here."

I nod, grateful for his kindness. "I appreciate that."

I take a sip of the coffee, letting it jolt me further awake. I need to pull myself together. There are too many questions swirling in my head, and I can't afford to let them consume me, not when I'm on the cusp of figuring out what happened to Camila.

It has been six years since I found out about her death. Six years of searching, digging, chasing every lead I could find. I've investigated the Whitmores from every angle, tried to expose them, tried to find anything that ties them to Camila's sudden end. But they're too powerful, too rich, and have everyone in their pockets—even the police commissioner. Every time I think I've uncovered something, it turns out to be another dead end.

Two thousand one hundred and ninety days of dead ends.

Part of me—the tired, worn-out part—wants to just accept the story they've fed everyone: that Camila killed herself. Yet there's a part of my mind that won't let me believe it, not for a second. I can't shake the feeling that the Whitmores had something to do with her death. I know they're involved. I can feel it in my bones.

Through my digging, I've managed to link some of the mysterious deaths of other women in Ebonridge to the Whitmores. There's a pattern, but without hard evidence, I can't prove it. No one believes me, or they're too afraid to even try.

The killings appear to be focused on young women. The victims are usually found in secluded spots where they wouldn't be immediately discovered, each crime scene with little physical evidence left behind.

But they all have the same cause of death: a slit throat.

I've poured over photos and reports, trying to piece everything together, but it has been a struggle, to say the least.

I don't know what it is about those murders that have me so intrigued, but I feel connected to them somehow.

They're meticulous and controlled, yet seemingly driven by impulses that break through that façade. The killings are precise and riddled with ritualistic aspects, suggesting a need to regain control.

I've always had a fascination with death and what causes people to act so heinously. It's ironic, given my appearance. You wouldn't think I'm into that kind of darkness. I dress in vibrant colors, my hair always perfectly styled, makeup carefully applied.

But looks can be deceiving.

Beneath the surface, there's a part of me that has always been drawn to the macabre, to the shadows that linger in the corners of the human psyche.

Since I was a teenager, I've been captivated by the darker aspects of human nature. I spent countless hours reading about infamous serial killers, studying their methods, trying to understand their motivations. There was something intriguing about the contrast between their outward normalcy and their hidden monstrosities. I wanted to know what made them tick, what pushed them over the edge, and if there was a way to predict and prevent such horrible acts.

Every insight, every breakthrough, brings me closer to understanding the depths of human depravity.

Sometimes, I question my own perversion. When I'm surrounded by images of brutality and violence, I can't help but wonder what it would feel like to step into the mind of the killer. To truly understand the darkness, would I need to embrace it myself?

I take another sip of coffee, feeling the caffeine start to kick in as Nathaniel and I walk to the office in comfortable silence.

As soon as we step inside the building, I'm ambushed by my colleague, Joshua, his face flushed with urgency.

"Valeria, did you check your email?" His voice is sharp, almost panicked.

I freeze mid-step, my heart skipping a beat. "No, not yet. Why? What happened?"

"Another woman was found dead. Three days ago, on the east side of Ebonridge at a Halloween party."

My breath catches in my throat. "Was it at the Whitmore estate?"

Joshua nods, his expression grim. "Yes."

My mind races, the blood draining from my face. I was at that party. "Tell me everything."

As we walk to my office, the corridors seem to stretch longer than usual. Finally, I push open my door and gesture for Joshua to follow.

"Close the door."

Joshua complies, and as soon as it clicks shut, he drops a file on my desk with a soft thud.

I sit down, my fingers trembling as I open the folder. The first thing I see is a photograph, and a gasp escapes my lips. I ruffle through the papers frantically, each image more horrifying than the last. My eyes widen as I recognize the person in the pictures.

This woman...I saw her in the first camera feed in the basement.

Joshua watches me intently. "Do you know her?"

I shake my head.

As I sift through the photographs, each image intensifies the sinking feeling in my stomach. I vividly remember the woman—the way she nervously glanced around the room, her discomfort palpable even through the grainy footage.

The murders always seem to circle the Whitmore property like vultures. Every time a body is discovered, it's always nearby, as if the estate itself draws the violence in, absorbing the darkness hiding beneath its polished surface.

I shake my head, feeling helpless.

"Valeria, what's wrong?" Joshua's voice breaks through my racing thoughts.

I meet his gaze, eyes wide with apprehension. "I was there," I confess.

Joshua's reaction is immediate; he plops down hard into the chair opposite my desk. "Oh shit," he mutters under his breath, running a hand through his hair. "Did you see anything? Anyone suspicious?"

I shake my head again, feeling the weight of guilt settle over me. "I remember details, but nothing definite. Did anyone come forward with information?"

Joshua sighs heavily, his shoulders slumping. "Someone did, but it was a dead end. A guest mentioned seeing the victim go upstairs with a man during the party. They came back down together, and everything seemed normal. No one recalls anything suspicious afterward. The next morning, she was found in the forest next to the property with a slit throat."

My mind races as I absorb the details, trying to piece together the puzzle.

Examining the rest of the photo, I notice her clothes. They look disheveled and torn, as if she had been running through the forest. Her dress is ripped in several places, the fabric snagged and shredded by branches. It's clear she was being chased.

This further proves my assumption that Camila's death reeks of something sinister. She was declared dead, but the circumstances surrounding her passing have always felt off. There was no official investigation, no signs of foul play. The Whitmores were quick to claim she committed suicide, but we've found nothing to prove it happened. It's like she just vanished, and that doesn't sit right with me.

The Whitmores are filthy rich, the kind of wealth that stretches back generations, with roots deep in this town. They own half of it, probably more, and their influence is everywhere. Money like that can buy a lot of things—silence, loyalty, cover-ups. I have no doubt they used it to bury whatever really happened to Camila, to make sure no one asks questions or digs too deep. After all, in a town like this, everyone has a price, and the Whitmores know exactly how to pay it.

It's infuriating knowing that they can just erase her like that, wipe away the truth with a few well-placed bribes. But I won't let them get away with it. Camila deserves justice, and I'm going to find out what really happened to her, no matter how many walls the Whitmores try to put up. Their money may buy a lot, but it won't buy my silence.

The mysterious stranger from the basement flashes through my mind.

Could she be involved? The thought is irrational. The killer's—or *killers'*—DNA, found at previous crime scenes, definitively point to a male perpetrator, but what if she was an accomplice?

Joshua watches me closely. "What are you thinking?"

"I saw a woman that night, near the woods. I need to find her. She might hold the key to this." I quickly give him a description of her and what she was wearing.

Joshua nods slowly. "Alright, we'll start there. I'll pull up footage from that area and see if we can identify her."

After Joshua leaves my office, I let out a slow, steadying breath.

As soon as the door clicks shut behind him, I turn to my computer, my fingers moving swiftly over the keyboard to bring up the security camera feed from the Halloween party. Joshua doesn't know that I've already been obsessively reviewing this footage for three days now, though initially for a completely different reason—pure infatuation.

At first, I scoured social media, sifting through hundreds of pictures and videos from the many socialites present, but there was no hint of her.

The internet was getting me nowhere, so I decided to use my own resources.

I contacted Marcus, a hacker employed by the agency. We'd worked together many times before on special projects and had a friendly, professional relationship, so I knew he'd comply without too many details.

He sent me the footage at record speed, and I didn't waste a second.

Now, as I click through the timestamps, my eyes scan each frame with a newfound purpose. There she is. Her presence in the footage sends a jolt through me. I study her movements, her interactions, searching for any clue that might connect her to the events of that tragic night, but nothing stands out.

But the answers are there, I know it. I just need to find the right angle, the right piece of the puzzle to make everything fall into place.

UNSOLVED

Valeria

I'm sitting in the back of my Uber, headed to Isabel's apartment.

Tonight, we're returning to the Whitmore estate, and I can't shake this gnawing anxiety. I offered to go alone this time, but Isabel insisted on coming with me. In a way, I'm relieved to have her by my side.

It has been two weeks since the Halloween party, and we're halfway into November. The holiday has passed, and the weather has started to cool, but the eerie vibes from Halloween still linger in the air, a haunting presence that hasn't quite left us. The leaves are falling, but there's a strange stillness, like the world is holding its breath.

I glance at my phone to check how far we are from Isabel's place: three minutes.

I open our chat.

Me: Come out now.

Isa: Yes, Mommy.

Me: Haha. Two minutes.

I chuckle and slip my phone back into my purse. Looking down at my outfit, I start to second-guess my choice—a check-ered pink skirt paired with a white and pink crop top. Maybe I should've gone with something less playful. I'm not sure what to expect, but if it's anything like the Halloween party, it's bound to be disturbing. A knot tightens in my stomach, my nerves making my hands slightly clammy.

The car stops, Isabel already waiting outside. As she hops into the back seat, I whistle.

"Wow. On time *and* dressed to impress," I tease.

Isa grins, giving me a playful wink. "What can I say? I'm a good listener. Do you think this outfit is too much?" she asks, gesturing to her purple tie-dye skirt and white crop tank.

I shake my head. "You look great, babe. I just hope whatever they have planned doesn't involve bending over or running."

She laughs. "Let's hope it's not hide and seek."

The mention of that game sends a shiver down my spine as I recall the memory of Halloween night. My body stiffens invol-untarily.

Isa notices and touches my arm gently. "What's wrong, Val?"

"What if it *is* hide and seek?" I murmur, my voice betraying my unease. "The girl I saw in those monitors was running, and it felt so...creepy."

"It was Halloween. *Everything*'s creepy on Halloween," Isabel says, trying to reassure me. "I doubt they'd do anything like that on a normal Saturday night."

I nod, but my eyes drift to the window, lost in thought. Soon, I'll be at the Whitmore estate again, searching for any clues about Camila's death. If she lived there, there must be something, some evidence of her disappearance. I'm deter-mined to find it, even if I have to sneak away and search on my own. Hopefully, no one catches me in the act.

In the six years I've been in Ebonridge, I've never found a way inside the Whitmore estate. It's frustrating—the family is impossibly secretive, their parties even more discreet. If you don't have an invitation from a Vanguard member or the family itself, you're not getting in, no matter how hard you try.

Isabel eventually landed a part-time job at Vanguard as a waitress, just to get us closer. Finally, this past Halloween, we got our first real chance. When Isabel told me she'd managed to schmooze one of the members into inviting us, I almost cried. After all this time, we finally had a foot in the door. Tonight is my second—maybe last—chance.

As we approach the estate, the atmosphere around us shifts, growing more somber. The trees seem to close in, their branches arching like twisted fingers over the narrow road.

"Thanks," I mutter to the Uber driver when he drops us off.

At the entrance, two men stand guard, their expressions unreadable. I instinctively step ahead of Isabel, protectiveness flaring up inside me. My heart pounds as one of them approaches us.

"Name?" he asks curtly.

"Uh, Valeria. This is Isabel."

Isabel chimes in smoothly. "Yes. The RSVP should be under my last name: Soto. The invitation was from Mr. Montclair."

I don't miss Isabel's slight flinch at the mention of his name. When I asked her if she could get us another invitation, I didn't expect her to reach out to the same man who had led her upstairs on Halloween. She assured me it was our only option, but guilt gnaws at me, remembering how scared I found her that night.

The guard nods and steps aside. "Right this way, *Mesdemoiselles*," he says, his voice dripping with an unsettling formality.

As we ascend the grand staircase, I take in the details of the mansion that were obscured by darkness the last time. The architecture is imposing, with archways that seem to stretch on endlessly. A chill runs through me, making my skin prickle. It reminds me of Gloomwood.

At the top, I reach for Isabel's hand, seeking some comfort in her presence.

We exchange a final, tense glance before stepping into the unknown.

"WELL, WHO DO WE HAVE HERE?" A SLEAZY VOICE SLITHERS FROM my right. The man speaking is tall and broad-shouldered, with slicked-back hair. His eyes are dark and predatory, raking over us with intensity.

Another man, leaner and a bit taller, cuts in. "Looks like fresh meat," he sneers, his tone dripping with malice. A maniacal laugh escapes his lips, sending a chill down my spine.

Isabel and I stand in the foyer, flanked by two men wearing the same eerie masks I'd seen at the Halloween party. It must be some sort of rule to attend these gatherings incognito, likely to protect their identities. The masks, with their hollow eyes, only add to the suffocating atmosphere.

Suddenly, a third man appears from the shadows. He's striking, with an aristocratic air, his blonde hair perfectly styled and his tailored suit fitting him like a glove. He exudes a cold, calculating charm as he steps forward. "I've never seen you here before, ladies." His voice is smooth but laced with condescension. He takes our hands, lifting them to his lips and planting a kiss on each of our knuckles. "I'm Theodore Whitmore, but you can call me Theo. These are my brothers, Maxwell and Julian."

Maxwell lets out a small chuckle. "Not actual brothers," he adds with a smirk.

Theodore turns to scowl at him—at least, I think it's a scowl beneath that mask. "Thanks for the clarification," he snaps.

Maxwell just laughs and shrugs while Julian remains silent, his eyes fixated on Isabel and me.

"What are your names?" Theo asks, his gaze lingering on Isabel a second too long. The others' eyes are on her too, their interest palpable. *What the hell is going on?*

Isabel shifts uncomfortably, her cheeks flushing a deep red. "My name is Isabel. This is Valeria," she says, her voice a bit shaky as she gestures to me.

Theo nods, a sinister smile spreading across his face. "Welcome to *Latibulum Noctis*," he announces, spreading his arms wide, as if to embrace the night itself. "Tonight, leave your inhibitions at the door and enter with an open mind. I promise we'll show you a good time." His grin is almost delirious.

"Follow me," he commands, turning to lead the way deeper into the house.

I take a deep breath, steeling myself for whatever lies ahead. No matter what happens tonight, I have to stay focused on why I'm here. If letting go of my inhibitions is what it takes to uncover the truth about Camila, then so be it. She's worth the risk.

As we follow the three men into the dark hallway, I lean over to Isabel, who still seems distracted. "You were enjoying the attention, weren't you?" I mumble with a teasing grin.

She shrugs, a mischievous glint in her eye, her lips curling into a small smile. "Maybe."

"You little slut," I whisper with a chuckle.

"Hey, I'm here for a good time, not a long time," she replies, her tone proud as she nudges me playfully.

I tug her closer. "As long as you promise to be safe."

"Yes, *Mommy*," she teases, her grin widening.

"Oh my God. Are you ever going to stop with that shit?" I groan, rolling my eyes.

"Nope!" she quips, clearly enjoying herself.

"Whatever. Just remember, if we get separated and you need help, text me our keyword," I remind her, my tone more serious now.

"Yes, I'll make sure to pull out my phone and text you while I'm being murdered," she says in a mockingly dramatic tone.

I stop in my tracks, shocked by her flippancy. "*Isabel Lucia Soto*. Be serious for two fucking seconds," I hiss, my heart pounding in my chest.

"Fine, fine. I'll make sure to reach out if anything looks sketchy," she concedes, her tone softening when she sees the worry in my eyes.

We round a corner and enter a grand hall, where more people are gathered, talking and drinking. It's an intimate party, but there are at least twenty other people here, most of them men in those spine-chilling masks. The sense of danger hangs thick in the air. We are *really* outnumbered.

A server glides over to us, holding a silver tray with flutes of champagne. The bubbles fizz enticingly in the crystal glasses, but something about the scene makes me hesitate. I exchange a glance with Isabel, who looks just as uncertain. Still, we each take a glass, the cold metal of the tray brushing against my fingers as I accept it. The waiter's face is expressionless, his eyes vacant, as if he's just another part of the decor.

With our drinks in hand, we scan the room. The other women present are a mixed crowd. Some hold themselves with a haughty air, their noses slightly upturned as they gaze down at us, as if being at a Whitmore party is some kind of exclusive privilege they've earned.

But others, hidden or standing awkwardly near the walls, paint a different picture. Their eyes dart nervously around the room, and they cling to their glasses as if for dear life. They look frightened, their faces pale and tense, as if they've been coerced into attending this event. I catch one girl's eye—she looks like she's barely out of her teens, her hand trembling as she brings her glass to her lips.

Suddenly, an older man with graying hair steps forward, commanding the room's attention with a loud, authoritative clearing of his throat. His suit is impeccably tailored, his posture straight, and there's an air of long-standing power around him.

The longer I stare at him, the more recognition hits. It's Lionel Whitmore, Camila's adoptive father. I'm rooted to the spot.

The conversations die down as everyone turns to face him, the room falling into a tense silence.

"Good evening, ladies and gentlemen," he begins, a hint of a smile playing on his lips. "Welcome to tonight's gathering. As always, it's a pleasure to see so many familiar faces...and a few new ones," he adds, his eyes briefly sweeping over Isabel and me, causing a shiver to run down my spine.

"For tonight's entertainment," he continues, his tone growing darker, "we have chosen a game both thrilling and exhilarating. I'm sure many of you are familiar with it." He pauses, letting the anticipation build, and I feel the room collectively hold its breath.

"We will be playing...hide and seek."

My heart drops, and I glance at Isabel, who is now visibly tense, her earlier bravado fading. Lionel's smile widens at the reaction his announcement elicits, and the men in the room exchange eager looks, their excitement barely contained.

"The rules are simple," he continues, his eyes gleaming with something almost sinister. "You hide, and when the clock strikes midnight, we seek. But be warned—those who are found...Well, let's just say that's when the real fun begins." His chuckle is low and menacing, and it reverberates through the room, chilling me to the core.

I grip Isabel's hand tightly, feeling the cool sweat on her

palm as we stand there, our nerves fraying with each passing second.

"Looks like we're in for a real treat," Isabel whispers.

The game might seem harmless in theory, but in this context, it feels ominous.

Mr. Whitmore, still standing in the center of the room, raises a glass in a toast. "To a night of thrills and surprises," he announces with a grin. "May the best hiders win."

His speech is followed by a chorus of muted laughter and a few nervous giggles. Isabel and I exchange a worried glance.

"Do you think we should stick together?" Isabel asks.

We watch as the guests scatter, disappearing down shadowy corridors.

"Definitely," I reply, trying to keep my own anxiety in check. "We need to stay close and keep an eye out for anything strange."

As we move deeper into the mansion, the sense of isolation becomes more pronounced.

We find ourselves in a room that appears to be a library, its shelves lined with ancient-looking books and dusty relics. The heavy air seems to press in on us, and the silence is occasionally broken by the distant sounds of footsteps and hushed voices.

"I'm starting to feel like we're in one of those old horror films," Isabel whispers.

"Please don't."

"What? I'm just saying. It feels like we're being hunted. I've seen this before."

"Isa," I groan, rolling my eyes. "Let's just keep moving and stay out of sight."

Isabel chuckles. "Okay, Mommy."

I grab a book from the shelf and toss it at her, narrowly missing. Her laughter only grows louder.

Grabbing her arm, I pull her along as we move through the

library, passing a grand fireplace. The mantle is cluttered with strange trinkets, framed portraits of grim-faced ancestors watching us from the walls. I spot a small door partially hidden behind a large leather chair and motion for Isabel to follow me.

We slip through and find ourselves in a narrow passageway. The walls are lined with old portraits that seem to watch us with disdainful eyes. It's cramped and the air is musty.

"Do you think this is a good place to hide?" Isabel asks.

"It's as good as any," I reply, trying to sound reassuring. "If anything feels off, we get out of here and regroup."

We huddle in the tight space, hoping no one finds us.

WE'VE BEEN HIDING FOR WHAT FEELS LIKE HOURS.

My legs are tucked up against my chest, but I don't dare move. I can feel Isabel beside me, her breathing slow and steady, though I know she's just as tense as I am. My heart hammers in my chest, and I close my eyes, willing it to quiet down.

The sound of a clock chimes unexpectedly. One, two, three... It echoes through the walls, each ring stretching the silence tighter. Twelve rings. Midnight. The signal.

Isabel places a hand on my arm, her grip tight.

I push myself up slowly, legs shaking as the blood rushes back into them. My muscles scream in protest, but there's no time to linger. The search begins now. My fingers tremble as I press them against the hidden latch we came through earlier. I slide the panel aside, just a crack, enough to peer out. Nothing. The room is empty.

Isabel leans forward, her hair brushing my arm, and I can hear her barely-there exhale of relief.

At that moment, footsteps echo in the near distance,

steadily approaching before halting abruptly. A tense silence follows, and I freeze, trying to remain as still as possible.

After a few seconds, the footsteps resume, moving away from us. I let out a slow exhale.

"Let's stay here a bit longer, then make our way back to the main hall. I need to start looking for clues."

Isabel nods, her eyes wide with unease.

But then, a group of masked men strides past us. My breath catches in my throat as I see the glint of metal in their hands—knives, long and wickedly sharp. They move with a predatory grace; their intentions clear in the way they hold their weapons.

Isabel's gasp slips out before she can stop it, and I lock in place, silently praying they didn't hear. To my great dismay, one of the men abruptly halts, turning slowly toward us. I feel Isabel's panic radiating off her as she presses herself against the wall.

As the man turns, my heart sinks. It's one of the brothers we met earlier, the one who introduced himself with that unnerving sneer—Theodore. His forehead scrunches behind the mask as he scans the area, suspicion flickering in his gaze.

Why are they carrying knives? The question pounds in my head, making it hard to think. This is supposed to be a game, but the way they're acting—like they're hunting—doesn't add up. *Was Isabel right?*

He seems to look right at us, and for a moment, I'm sure we've been spotted. But he shrugs it off, turning back to the others. They begin to walk away, their footsteps fading, but something's wrong. They vanish from view far too quickly. The corridor stretches out ahead of them—they should still be in sight, but it's as if they've disappeared into thin air.

"What the hell?" I whisper.

Before either of us can move, one of the brothers appears out of nowhere, his hand clamping down on Isabel's arm.

She screams, the sound piercing the eerie silence, and I

lunge forward, desperately trying to grab onto her. My fingers brush against hers, but he's too fast, dragging her with a chilling ease. Isabel kicks and struggles, her legs flailing as she tries to break free, but Theodore just laughs—a dark, cruel sound that fills me with dread.

"Let her go!" I yell, my voice raw with panic as I reach for her again, but it's too late. The other two brothers materialize from the shadows, each grabbing one of her legs, hoisting her up as if she weighs nothing.

"No! Isabel!" I cry out, chasing after them, my heart racing as I try to keep up. It's like they're moving faster than humanly possible, pulling her further and further away from me. "Why aren't you taking me too?" I shout, desperation and confusion knotting in my stomach.

A strong arm wraps around my waist, jerking me backward. A leather glove clamps over my mouth, muffling my startled yelp. I thrash wildly, but the grip is unyielding, and I'm pulled against a solid, immovable body.

Fear paralyzes me, but something about this hold is terrifyingly familiar. My body instinctively molds into my captor's, like I'm supposed to be there, and that realization makes my blood run cold. My breath comes in ragged gasps as I try to think of a way out, but my mind is a blur of panic.

The gloved hand tightens around my throat, the leather pressing against my skin, cutting off my air supply. I recognize this grip. It's *her*. It must be her.

My vision begins to blur as I struggle to breathe, to stay conscious, but my strength is fading. I wriggle against the hold, adrenaline surging through me, but my assailant is too powerful. Fear shoots through me, but there's an odd thrill too, an unexpected rush.

With the last bit of energy I can muster, I bite down hard on the fingers over my mouth. The person lets out a sharp hiss of pain, their grip loosening just enough for me to wrench myself free.

The world tilts as I spin, panic rising like bile in my throat as I come face-to-face with the woman from the basement. My next inhale falters as I take her in, the same skull mask covering half her face.

Her eyes, dark and penetrating, seem to bore into mine, sending prickles down my spine. Goosebumps rise on my skin despite the adrenaline coursing through me.

Our chests rise and fall in sync, the silence between us heavy with tension. Time seems to stand still as we size each other up.

"Come with me," she says after a few silent beats.

UNSOLVED

8

Valeria

I'm too stunned to respond.

I back away instinctively, but she steps forward, her gloved hand reaching out as if to reclaim what she believes is hers.

My fingers find the familiar shape of my pink, pointed kubotan in the waistband of my skirt, and I grip it discreetly for reassurance. I assumed they wouldn't allow the guests to come in with actual weapons, so this was the next best thing. I tighten my hold on the stick, ready to defend myself, if necessary, but the masked woman doesn't budge.

Just when I begin to contemplate my next move, she surprises me. In one swift motion, she whips out a knife and presses it against my throat, her eyes gleaming with a dangerous glint.

For a moment, I freeze, caught off guard by her suddenness, but anger surges within me.

I pivot, twisting her around and pinning her against the wall.

My weapon is now at her neck, mirroring her threat. We're locked in a deadly dance, each holding the other at bay.

"What do you want from me?" I manage to choke out.

I meet her gaze head-on, searching for any hint of weakness, but instead, I find a glimmer of amusement in her dark eyes, as if she's relishing the confrontation.

"You picked the wrong person to mess with," I hiss.

She doesn't answer, but her eyes crinkle with a smile.

Finally, she speaks again, her voice steady despite the stick at her throat. "You're more cunning than I thought" she admits, a hint of admiration in her tone. "But you still have nothing on me."

The stranger's leg sweeps under mine with a grace that almost makes me miss what's happening. The ground slips away beneath my feet, and there's a rush of air as I tilt backward, my heart leaping into my throat. But before panic can even set in, I'm caught.

Her arm is there like it knows exactly where I'll land. She guides me down as if we're in some kind of twisted dance, her grip firm but not bruising.

I blink up at her, half in shock, half in awe.

Before I can do anything more, the cold steel of her knife presses against my chest, poking a hole through the fabric of my top. I gasp, my skin erupting in goosebumps.

Her eyes bore into mine and the edge of her blade rests against my skin.

My chest heaves with rapid breaths, the rush of fear mingling inexplicably with a surge of something else entirely.

I'm not supposed to feel this way—pinned beneath a knife, my life hanging in the balance. But beneath the fear, there's a dangerous thrill that courses through me like electricity.

The tension between us crackles like static in the air.

I should be terrified, fighting for my life against a masked assailant. Instead, a part of me wants to challenge her further, to see just how far she'll go.

She leans in closer, the blade pressing lightly against my skin.

I inhale sharply. "You don't scare me."

Her breath warms my ear despite the fabric of her thin mask. "What are you really afraid of then, Valeria?" she taunts, her voice a seductive lure, and I freeze at the mention of my name.

She knows who I am.

In that moment, the line between fear and arousal blurs.

She fixes her gaze on me, and slowly, almost reluctantly, removes the mask.

I'm momentarily stunned into silence.

The dim light of the passageway accentuates her features.

Her beauty is disarming, almost hypnotic. I find myself unable to look away.

Her nose is perfectly sculpted, her lips plump and inviting. I'm drawn to the subtle curve of her mouth, the way they part ever so slightly as she smirks at me. The smile, both mocking and enticing.

A glint of metal catches my eye—a tongue piercing—and I lick my own lips subconsciously as my gaze lingers on hers.

My whole body shivers involuntarily.

How can I be so entranced by someone who's holding a knife to my throat? I'm truly questioning my sanity.

"You're not what I expected," she remarks casually, her voice a velvet whisper. "You're even better."

Her fingers toy with the handle of the knife as I struggle to find my voice, torn between the urge to retreat and the inexplicable desire to get closer.

"Who are you?" I swallow hard, my pulse racing as I search for words that elude me.

She leans in, her breath brushing against my cheek. "Does it matter?"

"Yes," I breathe out.

She shakes her head. "Just follow me."

"Why should I trust you?" I manage to ask, turmoil rising within me.

"Because you're in danger," she replies simply. "And I'm the only one who can help you."

I weigh her words carefully, assessing the sincerity in her eyes. The Whitmores and Camila loom in the back of my mind. She could hold the key to unraveling their secrets. Or is she merely another player in this dangerous game?

I guess I'll have to find out.

9

Ronnie

I finally push myself off Valeria, the adrenaline still coursing through my veins. I can feel the tension in my muscles as I sheath my knife, sliding it back into its holder around my thigh.

My hand hovers above Valeria, ready to help her up, but she shrugs me off.

"I don't need your help," she spits. "Nor do I need your protection. I don't even know you!" she argues, a defiant glint returning to her eyes as she squares her shoulders.

A soft chuckle escapes my lips. "You might be a little warrior, but you don't know what you're up against. We're alone here, Valeria. Proceed with caution," I say, noticing the slight tilt of her head and the way her eyes hold mine, daring me. Her skirt is hiked up, and the sight of her bare thighs makes my breath catch.

As she moves to adjust her clothing, her eyes meet mine.

Her hair is tousled, a few strands framing her face, and her cheeks are tinged with a rosy hue.

My eyes follow the angles of her face until they reach her lips.

A strange wave of familiarity hits me, so strong, it nearly knocks the breath out of me. It's like I already know how they feel—soft, warm—and, God, the taste of her tongue flashes in my mind like a memory that shouldn't be there. The feeling is so vivid, it's unsettling. I tear my eyes away, shaking it off, but the pull lingers, like something I've forgotten but can't fully grasp.

Fuck, fuck, fuck.

I'm so entranced by Valeria, I begin to wonder if it was a bad idea to get involved with her outside of observing her through screens. Watching her from a distance, through the safety of a monitor, had seemed much simpler, safer. But here she is, so real.

Get a grip, Verónica. All the stalking and digging I've been doing is messing with my head. I've gone too deep, watching her every move, reading into things that probably aren't even there. But still, the sensation won't leave me, clinging to me.

Valeria straightens, smoothing her skirt with a confident flick of her wrist. Then, she turns on her heels and tries to walk away, but I grab onto her arm.

"Not so fast," I say.

I step closer, and the space between us crackles with energy. Her inhales are sharp, and I feel the warmth radiating from her body, so close, I can almost feel her heartbeat.

"You don't know what I'm capable of," she taunts, her lips curling into a daring smile. "Now, if you'll excuse me, I need to find Isabel. I can't just stay here—"

"Relax. They won't hurt her."

Valeria scoffs. "How can you say that? This place obviously isn't what it seems, and they had knives. *Knives!*" Her voice cracks.

"I've been watching them. They don't hurt women. They just...like to have fun with them."

"*Fun,*" she repeats, as if the word tastes bitter in her

mouth. "Isabel's out there, probably terrified, and I'm stuck here with...with *you*, whoever you are. I need to check if she's okay."

I let out a pent-up breath. She's not going to make this easy. I don't move, my gaze holding hers with an intensity that makes her coil into herself. "Valeria, you need to listen to me. Isabel will be fine, but if you go after her, you might not meet the same fate."

Her eyes widen. "What do you mean?"

"The Whitmores aren't to be trusted. These game nights are dangerous."

She narrows her eyes at me, crossing her arms over her chest, causing her perfect tits to push upward. "Then why are you here?"

I mirror her stance. "I'm not here as a guest. Like I said, I've been watching this family for a while now. Those boys might be harmless, but the others aren't. So, you either stick with me or end up dead."

Valeria freezes, my words finally sinking in. "Fuck. *Camila*," she mutters.

"Who's Camila? I thought your friend's name was Isabel."

She shakes her head, as if to dispel her thoughts. "Uh. Yeah. Camila is...an old friend. I was hoping I could find out what happened to her tonight."

"I could help," I offer, noticing a glint of silver catching the light.

My eyes land on the butterfly necklace around Valeria's neck. *My* necklace. It suits her perfectly. Without thinking, my hand reaches out, fingers brushing against the cool metal.

As I touch it, Valeria's eyes meet mine, and for a second, I'm worried she'll see everything I'm feeling written all over my face. My pulse quickens, and I swallow hard.

"Are you sure? I mean...this place," she says.

I reach up to brush a stray lock of hair from her face, my

fingers grazing her cheek. Valeria's breath hitches. "Yes, princesa."

Her gaze darts to the floor. "Okay," she cedes.

I grab Valeria's hand, feeling her pulse quicken through her skin. She's nervous.

"Come on," I whisper. Her eyes are wide, filled with questions she hasn't asked yet. She nods, trusting me even though she has every reason not to.

The corridor is narrow, damp, the kind of place that makes your skin crawl if you think about it too much. But I've studied the entire layout of the mansion, so I know the way.

I keep moving, one foot in front of the other, leading her through the darkness.

It's then I hear voices—too close for comfort. I pull Valeria sharply to the side, pressing us both against the cold stone wall. The space is too damn tight, barely enough room for the two of us.

"Shhh," I say. The voices get closer, and I can tell Valeria's holding her breath, trying not to make a sound.

It's just a couple of drunk men who have no idea how close they are to us. We stay frozen until I'm sure they're gone, and then I nod to Valeria. "Let's go." We slip out of our hiding spot and continue down the passage, quicker this time. She's keeping up, but I can feel her fear, the way her hand shakes slightly in mine. I tighten my grip, hoping to steady her.

Finally, we reach the end, facing an old elevator. It's rusted, barely functional, and looks as if it hasn't been used in ages, but it's our only way up.

"This way," I say, pulling open the barrier.

I can see the hesitation in her eyes. "Are you sure about this?"

"I know it looks bad, but it's the only way up without being seen. Trust me."

She takes a deep breath and steps inside, the floor creaking under her weight. I follow, closing the gate behind us. The space is tiny, claustrophobic, but I push the feeling down and focus on the controls, trying to remember the sequence.

"Why are you even looking into the Whitmores?" Valeria asks, her voice cutting through the silence.

I freeze, my fingers hovering over the buttons.

"The Whitmores have done things—terrible things—and they've been getting away with it for years because no one has the power to stop them." My voice shakes with anger I can barely contain.

"Yeah. I think they have something to do with Camila's disappearance," she mutters.

The elevator lurches into motion, the old gears groaning in protest. Valeria grips the railing, her knuckles white.

"We were orphans, Isabel, Camila, and me. When Camila turned seventeen, she was adopted by the Whitmores. I was younger... I had no way of keeping in touch with her, so when I left the orphanage two years later, I started looking for her." Valeria leans back against the cold metal wall, staring down as if she's watching memories play out on the floor. "They took her in like they were doing her some big favor, but she didn't last long. They claimed she tried to run away and committed suicide."

My head snaps up to look at her. Valeria's still talking, so I don't interrupt.

"They said there was no foul play, that she wasn't happy and just couldn't handle it anymore. But Camila was never suicidal," Valeria continues, her voice growing firmer. "She was quiet, almost mute, and she kept to herself, but she wasn't broken. She just needed time, and they never gave it to her."

Valeria's hand goes to the butterfly necklace around her neck. She touches it gently like it's some kind of lifeline. "We bonded over butterflies," she says, and there's something soft, almost tender, in her voice. "That's how we got close. That's how I fell for her."

Her words hit me like a punch to the gut. I just stare at her, trying to process everything she said.

"That's why I've been wearing this necklace ever since you gave it to me," she murmurs, her fingers still tracing the pendant. "It's like I'm carrying a part of her with me. But why did you give it to me?"

I look down, my thoughts swirling. Why did I give it to her? I didn't know the story then, didn't know what it meant. "I have no idea," I admit, feeling an odd vulnerability in the confession. "I just felt like you needed to have it. And now, hearing all this, maybe I understand why."

The elevator jolts, and I grab onto the railing, steadying myself. Valeria does the same, but her eyes are far away, most likely lost in thought. I want to say something to comfort her, but the words just don't come.

"Do you still love her?" I spit out, regretting the question as soon as it slips from my mouth.

Valeria nods. "I do. But I've made peace with her absence. I just need to find out what really happened to her. I owe her that much."

The elevator shudders to a stop, the doors creaking open with a metallic whine that echoes down the hallway ahead. The corridor stretches out in front of us, lined with old wooden doors, each one closed.

"If we're going to do this together, I should at least know your name," Valeria says from behind me as I step out.

Turning back to look at her, I answer, "You can call me Ronnie."

"Ronnie," she repeats. Hearing her speak my name in her sweet voice makes me want to hear her moaning it in my ear. *Stat.*

"It's short for Verónica," I add.

She nods as if absorbing the information. "I've never seen you around. I mean…before the Halloween party. That was you, right?"

"Yes," I say with a deep breath. "You shouldn't have been there."

Valeria scoffs. "Why not? You were there too."

"Not in the same capacity," I retort.

She rolls her eyes. "We were both there for a reason," Valeria sneers. "But I'm actually interested in knowing why you were in the basement then proceeded to watch me and Isabel from the tree line like a stalker," she continues, meeting my gaze head-on.

I'm walking down the hallway backward now. "A stalker, huh?" I say, eyes narrowed as I abruptly halt my steps, causing her to stop right in front of me. My lip grazes her ear as I lean forward. "Is that what you really think, princesa?

Ignoring my question, she backs away and lets out a growl of frustration. "Just answer the question."

My lip curls upward. "And what if I was? Would you be scared now?" I whisper in her ear, getting close again. Valeria's arms erupt in goosebumps as my breath touches her skin, but she doesn't falter and keeps up her tough façade.

"You do look really pretty in the mornings, though," I tease.

Valeria's expression shifts as she processes my words slowly, connecting the dots with a sudden realization. The color drains from her face. "What the fuck?" she whisper-yells. "You've been watching me?" Valeria's voice is sharp as she takes a step back, her fists clenched at her sides.

I hold her gaze steadily, my expression neutral. "I had to keep an eye on you—for research purposes."

Valeria shakes her head incredulously. "Watching me without my knowledge is *illegal!*" Her voice rises a tad.

I remain composed, unmoved by her accusations. "I see it

differently," I respond calmly, my confidence unwavering. "I had my reasons."

Valeria's fists loosen slightly, her anger giving way to a sense of incredulity. "You don't see how wrong that is?" she asks, her voice edged with disbelief.

I shrug nonchalantly, a hint of a smile playing at the corner of my lips. "Maybe not from where I stand," I admit unapologetically. "But I understand if you don't feel the same."

Valeria's jaw clenches as her hand reaches back. In one, swift movement, she grabs the kubotan stick from her waistband and charges at me.

She lunges forward as I grab my knife from its holder, and she strikes at me with precision. Goddamn. She's actually trying to hurt me.

With a sudden twist, I manage to deflect Valeria's strike, seizing her by the throat and slamming her against the wall. Her breath comes out as a wheeze as I press the knife to her throat, teasing the chain around her neck with the blade. "Minha borboleta linda. I told you not to try me."

Breathing heavily, our faces mere inches apart, we lock eyes. Valeria struggles against my grip, but I'm not letting her go. I love seeing her at my mercy.

Sensing an opportunity, I wrench the kubotan stick from her grasp.

Before Valeria can react, I spin her around, pushing her over the hallway table forcefully. The trinkets sitting on top clatter to the ground, and I don't even care that someone might hear us. I dare them to come.

A loud gasp escapes Valeria's lips as the front of her body thuds on the wooden top. Lifting her skirt, I tear her underwear away in a single, forceful motion.

Her sweet smell invades the air, and I close my eyes momentarily.

"Fuck, princesa. You're going to be the reason for a hundred deaths once I get a taste of you," I groan, not able to resist any longer.

Grabbing her wrists, I secure them behind her back, tying them with a piece of rope I had in my pocket. Then, I sink my fingers into her luscious blonde hair and jerk her head back with enough force to pull her lips apart so I can stuff the torn fabric of her thong in her mouth.

"Stay put," I order before I drop to my knees behind her like I'm getting ready for prayer.

Only this is *way* better.

I spread Valeria's ass cheeks, and she draws in a breath. "Ronnie, what are you doing?" she mumbles through her gag.

"Teaching you a fucking lesson," I grit out.

I press the pink kubotan stick firmly against her slick folds, and the metal slips. "Foda-se, princesa. You're soaked."

My mouth salivates at the thought of her wetness coating my tongue.

Slowly, I tease her pussy with the stick until the tip slips inside. Valeria lets out a mewl, which turns me on tenfold. I need to taste her.

Without a moment's hesitation, I push further inside her. Valeria's body jerks forward at the intrusion, and she lets out a yelp that carries both pain and pleasure.

At the same time, I stick my tongue out, letting the metal of my piercing glide over her swollen clit. Valeria knees buckle on contact. "Oh my God," she mumbles.

I moan as soon as her arousal hits my tastebuds. "Jesus. You are a fucking delicacy."

It's right then that I realize Valeria has to be mine.

UNSOLVED

10

———

Valeria

When Ronnie sticks the torn-up thong into my mouth, I instantly taste my arousal, and it makes me even wetter.

The feeling of her barbell stroking my clit causes my legs to shake beneath me. *Holy shit.* I've never experienced this amount of pure pleasure.

My eyes roll back, and I moan as my body shifts on the tabletop.

Pushing my ass toward Ronnie, I moan through the cotton of my panties.

She chuckles and speaks directly into my center, causing my breath to catch in my throat. "I'm showing you what it means to mess with someone like me, princesa." She sucks my clit, swirling her tongue, and my knees buckle. "To fight someone like me," she adds, pushing the kubotan stick further into my pussy. "To *fuck* someone like me."

Ronnie's words cause a rush of heat to surge through my body, my heart pounding wildly in my chest.

I don't know this woman, don't know what her intentions are, but I can't seem to think straight around her. My body acts of its own accord, ignoring the logical part of my brain that warns this might be dangerous. But I don't feel scared around Verónica.

On the contrary—I'm the most alive I've ever felt.

Every moment I've spent in her presence has been electric, and my senses are heightened in ways I never thought possible. The thrill of being near her outweighs any caution, and it's fucking intoxicating.

Ronnie's tongue runs laps around my clit as she gently maneuvers the kubotan inside me, and I feel my climax bubbling to the surface.

She devours me like a woman starved, and I can barely hold myself up, gripping the table desperately to stay up.

She pulls out the weapon and replaces it with two fingers, hooking them downward to apply pressure to my G-spot.

My arousal drips down my thighs, and I can only imagine how wet Ronnie's face must be. The thought amplifies every sensation.

"You're making such a mess, Valeria. *Fuck*," Ronnie grunts, temporarily removing her mouth from my mound to lick up my thighs. When she makes beckoning movements with her fingers inside my pussy, my mind is consumed by the sheer pleasure coursing through me. Consumed by *her*.

The feeling is overwhelming, and I lose myself entirely in the moment. I try to speak, to tell her I'm close, but it comes out as a whimper.

"Yes, butterfly. Vem-te para mim." *Come for me*, she groans, fucking me hard and steady with her hand.

She's speaking to me in what sounds like Portuguese, and the way the words roll off her tongue only turns me on more. I can't fully understand what she's saying, but I don't even care— it's just so *hot*.

Slowly, she swirls her piercing over my swollen nub, and

my breath catches. "Oh, fuck, I'm coming," I cry out, but it's muffled.

Within a few seconds, I come hard, my body trembling with the intensity of my orgasm.

My limbs feel heavy, every muscle in my body exhausted as I come down from the high.

With a gentle motion, Ronnie removes the thong from my mouth, her fingers brushing my lips, and stuffs it in her pocket.

As I taste the air again, Ronnie's voice reaches me. "Foste incrível. Mal posso esperar para que sejas minha." *You were incredible. I can't wait for you to be mine.*

Before I can fully process her words, her hand slides to my nape, her grip firm yet tender. She pulls me close, and our lips meet in a passionate kiss, her mouth claiming mine with an intensity that makes my heart race anew.

Fireworks explode in my veins, leaving me breathless. Ronnie's lips move against mine with both urgency and tenderness, her tongue teasing mine, deepening the kiss. The world fades away, leaving only the two of us.

Every touch of her lips, every brush of her tongue, sends waves of pleasure coursing through me all over again.

With a gentle motion, she unties the rope from around my wrists, and the moment the string loosens, I roll them, enjoying my renewed sense of freedom.

Then, she reaches between my legs and swipes her fingers through my slit, gathering a coat of my arousal. "Goddamn, Val. Isto é tudo para mim?" *Is this all for me?*

My body responds instinctively, pressing closer to her, craving more of the connection that makes me feel so alive. As the kiss continues, I lose myself in her.

Ronnie pulls away, rubbing the pads of her fingers all over my lips, spreading my wetness over my mouth.

"Taste yourself, princesa," she whispers into my ear. *Oh,*

God. Her voice is so fucking attractive, like a magnet drawing me in and making my skin tingle.

She pushes her fingers into my mouth, and it instinctively opens, letting me taste the tanginess of my cum.

I suck on them, Ronnie's eyes almost rolling behind her head from the act, then bite down. She hisses in pain. "Shit, Val," she says with a chuckle. "Don't bite me too hard. Eu sou capaz de gostar dessa merda." *I might actually like that shit.*

Her mouth lands on mine again, and I melt into her embrace once more.

When we finally pull away, both breathless, I manage to murmur, "Let me return the favor," between lingering kisses.

Ronnie leans into me, shaking her head. "I'm selfish and want to enjoy the taste of your pretty cunt for the rest of the night."

Her rejection only makes me want her more. "Ronnie," I whine.

Ronnie's eyes darken. "I love it when you say my name, princesa." Her gaze smolders as it locks onto mine.

She grabs my hand, guiding it down her pants. I gasp when I reach her warmth.

"See what you do to me, butterfly? I want you; there's no denying it," she explains as my fingers explore her wetness. Ronnie's breath hitches ever-so-slightly, but her words don't falter. "But next time, I want to take my time exploring every inch of your body. And right now, we need to keep moving before we're caught."

11

Ronnie

Fuck.

I curse myself for getting so wrapped up in Valeria. What the hell am I doing? Fingering her in the hallway during some twisted game of hide-and-seek? It's reckless, stupid.

I need to get the fuck away from Valeria. *Now*.

I shouldn't be losing focus like this. I'm supposed to be investigating the Whitmores and these damn murders, not playing with fire. I'm here to bring them down, not get tangled up in Valeria's messy past. Offering to help her dig up information on her lost lover—what was I thinking? She's a distraction. Every time I get close to her, I lose sight of why I'm here.

But I can't stop.

The taste of her perfect cunt is lingering on my tongue, and all I want to do is find a room and finish what we started. I'm uncomfortably wet, and I blame the blonde, girly pop bombshell standing in front of me. A light sheen of sweat slickens her forehead, her chest expanding with every breath, her mouth slightly parted, still swollen from our kiss.

I'm screwed.

Valeria looks back at me. "Are you coming?"

I shake my head to dispel my thoughts. "Do you even know where you're going?"

Just as she's about to answer, a figure emerges from the shadows.

UNSOLVED

12

R onnie takes a step forward, and that's when I see a man stepping out of the shadows like a nightmare come to life. In his hand, he's holding a large knife, the blade streaked with red.

"What the fuck?" I breathe, my voice trembling.

He doesn't say a word; he just tilts his head slightly, studying us, as if deciding what to do next. Then, he starts toward us, slow and deliberate, the knife catching the light with each step.

"Run!" Ronnie yells, grabbing my arm. I don't need to be told twice.

We take off, our footsteps echoing loudly in the large corridor. The hallway twists and turns, narrowing in places, the old doors passing by in a blur. I glance at them, and a chill runs down my spine.

"These doors—I saw them on the monitors on Halloween!" I gasp, but there's no time to stop, no time to think.

The man's footsteps are growing louder behind us, closer with every second. We turn another corner, but before I can register what's happening, Ronnie is yanked backward with terrifying force.

"Ronnie!" I scream, my heart lurching as I see the man pulling her down to the floor.

She hits the ground hard, and the knife in his hand glints as he raises it high. I freeze for a split second, terror paralyzing me, but then I see Ronnie fighting back, thrashing and kicking with everything she has. She manages to pull out her knife, slashing at his arm. Blood splatters everywhere, dark and thick, but it doesn't stop him. He snarls in pain, his mask slipping just enough for me to see part of a twisted, scarred face.

I watch in horror as the man's hand clamps down on Ronnie's throat, squeezing with brutal force. She's gasping for air, and a wave of helplessness crashes over me. I reach into my pocket, my fingers closing around the kubotan, but I know it's useless against him.

Desperately, I scan the hallway, my eyes landing on a small ceramic statue on a nearby table. I rush to grab it—a bust of some old figure, heavy and solid in my hand. I turn back just in time to see the man tightening his grip around Ronnie's neck, her face turning a terrifying shade of red.

"No!" I scream, running back to them. I swing the statue down with all my strength, smashing it against the back of his head. The impact is sickening, the sound of ceramic shattering mingling with the crunch of bone. Blood sprays as the man bellows in pain, but I don't stop. I hit him again and again, each blow more savage than the last.

Blood pours from the gash in his skull. His body jerks and twitches, but he doesn't let go of Ronnie, his fingers still wrapped around her. She's struggling, clawing at his hand.

With one final swing, I bring the statue down as hard as I can. Shards fly everywhere, and the man's body finally goes limp. He collapses on top of Ronnie, his blood flooding the floor around us.

I drop the broken pieces of the statue and stumble back, gasping for breath. The man is dead. My heart is pounding so hard, I can barely hear anything else.

I watch as Ronnie pushes the man's body off her, rolling to her side and coughing, gasping for air. The hallway is eerily silent now, save for the sound of our ragged breathing. The smell of death hangs heavily around us.

As I stand there, trembling, I look down at my hands covered in blood. It drips from my fingers, soaking into the fabric of my pink skirt, staining everything. For the first time in my life, I understand what it feels like to be depraved.

I've never come close to killing anyone before, but when I brought that statue down, again and again, something broke inside me. There was a rush—an unexpected high that flooded my veins, a feeling of power that made me unable to stop, even when I should have. It only pushed me further, drove me to keep going until his body was nothing but a broken, bleeding mass on the floor.

And now...

Now, I can't stop shaking.

I stagger back, choking on air that feels too heavy to breathe. The realization of what I've done crashes over me like a wave, and I feel sick. My legs give out beneath me, and I collapse onto the blood-soaked floor, tears streaming down my face.

I'm terrified of what I did, of what I felt, the thrill of it. It's as if I was living inside the mind of a killer—and for a moment, I liked it.

The thought sends a shudder through my whole body, and I sob, my hands trembling as I press them to my face. The blood smears across my skin, but I can't stop the flood of tears. I glance down at my clothes, once a soft pink, now drenched in deep red. The color seeps into everything, staining me in ways I'm not sure I can ever wash clean.

"Valeria," I hear Ronnie's voice, strained and hoarse, but it feels distant, like it's coming from another world.

"I couldn't stop," I whisper through my sobs. "I... couldn't...stop."

Ronnie crouches beside me, her face pale, still bruised from the fight. She doesn't say anything; she just wraps her arms around me, pulling me close. I cling to her, my body shaking uncontrollably.

"Hey," Ronnie whispers, holding me tighter. "You did what you had to. You saved us. Don't think about it right now, okay? Just breathe."

After a few moments, I finally gather myself, wiping the blood and tears from my face. My heart is still racing, but I push down the nausea rising in my throat. I can't fall apart now.

Ronnie helps me to my feet. "We need to keep moving before someone else finds us," she says.

I nod and let her lead me away from the crime scene. Each step feels heavier than the last, but I force myself to keep walking. Ronnie's pace is quick, her eyes scanning our surroundings. My mind is still spinning, but she breaks the silence.

"So, tell me more about Camila," she asks, glancing back at me. She's trying to distract me.

I swallow hard, trying to focus on the question. *Camila.* I have to think about Camila, not the blood, not the man I just killed.

"We—" I clear my throat, swallowing hard. "She was my first love."

Ronnie tenses. It's subtle at first, the way her shoulders stiffen as she walks, her fingers twitching slightly at her sides, but then it deepens. Her jaw tightens. I pause mid-sentence, watching her carefully. This isn't jealousy—I mean, we just met.

But Ronnie doesn't acknowledge the change in her demeanor.

We reach the end of the hallway, and we approach a large staircase leading to another floor. The steps look freshly polished, the banister smooth and gleaming. It's a stark contrast to the nightmare below. This part of the mansion looks like it's lived in, the doors no longer worn and old.

Ronnie glances around, ensuring no one's in sight. "Let's go."

We ascend the staircase quietly when I suddenly remember Isabel.

I fumble for my phone, pulling it out of my pocket, my fingers shaking. I check for messages—nothing. My heart sinks: Isabel hasn't texted me. No keyword. No sign. My stomach twists with panic. Maybe Ronnie was wrong. Maybe she *is* in danger.

"What's wrong?" Veronica asks.

"Isabel hasn't messaged me. You said they wouldn't hurt her, but what if she's phone-less? What if she *can't* text me?"

Ronnie pauses, turning to face me, her expression softening. "I told you; those guys aren't going to hurt her. They're probably just keeping her busy. But I get it—you're scared. After everything, it makes sense."

I bite my lip, torn. Part of me wants to run and find Isabel, to make sure she's safe. But after what we've just been through, after what I did...I don't know if I can do this without Ronnie. I don't *want* to do this without her.

I shove my phone back in my pocket and take a deep breath. *She's fine,* I try to convince myself.

We continue going upstairs, and when we reach the top, Ronnie picks a door at random, slowly pushing it open.

What we see freezes us in place.

It's a bedroom, neutral but dark. The walls are a deep, muted gray, with subtle pops of color here and there. A vase of dried flowers sits on a dresser, their petals faded and brittle. But what really catches my eye are the butterflies. Images of them cover the walls, intricately drawn, their delicate wings captured mid-flight. They're everywhere, on every surface, every wall. The sight of them sends a chill through me.

Mounted right above the bed is a wooden sign, the carved letters spelling out a name in delicate cursive: *Camila.*

A lump forms in my throat that I can't swallow down. I feel it like a punch to the gut. This was where she slept, where she lived, where she dreamed.

Ronnie steps inside, her eyes narrowing as she takes it all in. "This is her room," she says quietly, like she's speaking the thought aloud to confirm it for herself.

I don't answer her. I can't. I feel frozen, my gaze glued to the name above the bed, my mind reeling. Camila is everywhere in this room—the butterflies, the subtle darkness, the quiet way it all feels like a part of her. It's almost like she's still here, haunting the space.

I step further inside, my fingers brushing against the back of a chair by the bed. The wood is cool beneath my skin, and I imagine her sitting there, brushing her hair, silent as ever. The image makes my chest tighten.

Ronnie's jaw clenches as she takes in the room again. "I've been here before."

13

Ronnie

The moment I stepped into the room; a strange feeling hit me. It's like I've stayed here, maybe even slept in this bed. I can't explain it, but it's familiar. I can feel it in my soul, like a memory trying to resurface, just out of reach.

I sit on the edge of the bed, my fingers brushing over the soft sheets. A shiver runs down my spine. "I've been here before," I mutter, more to myself than to Valeria, but she catches it.

"What do you mean?" Valeria asks, waiting for me to explain something I don't even understand myself.

"I don't know." I shake my head, my hands gripping the edge of the mattress. "It feels like I've been in this room before, slept in this bed. But that doesn't make any sense, does it?" My voice cracks at the end, frustration bubbling up. Nothing about this should feel familiar, yet it does.

Valeria doesn't respond right away. Instead, she stretches out next to me, staring up at the ceiling. She lifts her arms above her head, the long line of her body relaxed, and I try to focus, to shake the feeling creeping up my spine. But then, I see it: a tattoo, small script along her ribcage, just under her shirt.

Mors tua, vita mea.

My breath catches. The world tilts on its axis.

The sentence burns into my memory from a time I didn't even know I'd forgotten.

I stare at it, my mouth suddenly dry. My heart starts racing, pounding so loud, I can hear it in my ears. "Val," I say, my voice barely a whisper, "when did you get that tattoo?"

Valeria glances down at me, confused. "I've had it for years. Why?"

I can't speak, can't move. Every single forgotten memory hits me at once, a rush of images, feelings—everything. My vision blurs as the memories flood in, an unstoppable tidal wave.

Valeria sits up, her eyes wide now. "Verónica, what's going on? You look like you've seen a ghost. Did you hear something?"

I can't answer. I'm shaking, my hands trembling as I grip the bed harder. My throat feels tight like it's closing. Everything starts falling into place, and I'm terrified.

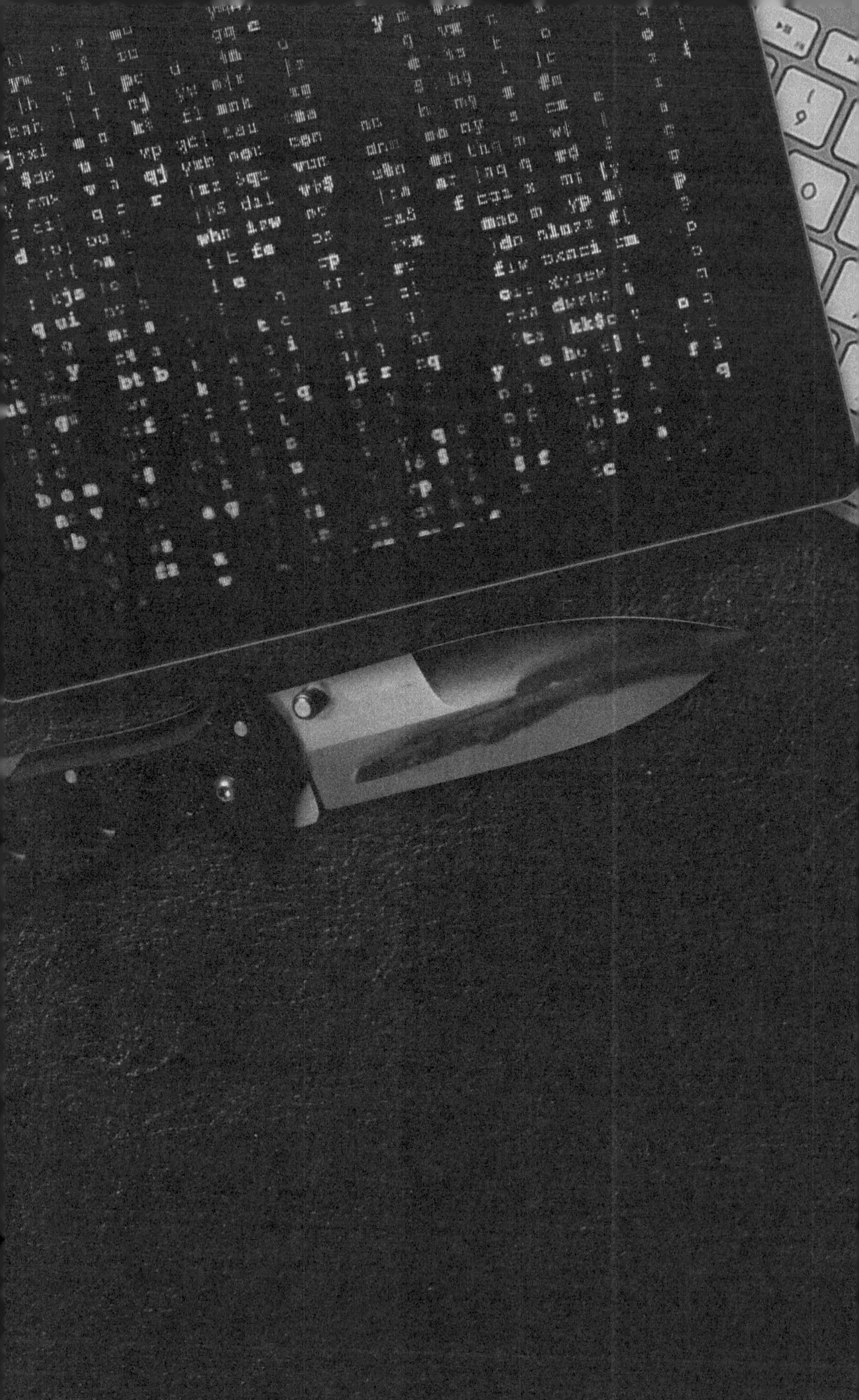

14

———

Ronnie

17 YEARS OLD

The unfamiliar softness of the mattress beneath me is completely disorienting. The silky sheets tangle around my limbs as I blink in the morning light filtering through the sheer curtains. For a moment, I can't remember where I am.

Gloomwood had always been so different—everything cold and gray, the walls made of rough, unyielding stone, the constant sound of the sisters shuffling outside our doors. There had been the ever-present hum of the other girls' chatter, muffled but never absent, but here, in the Whitmore mansion, there's nothing but silence. *Too* much silence. The stillness seeps into me, amplifying the loneliness I've carried since arriving here months ago. This place, no matter how beautiful, makes me feel hollow, like I'm slowly fading into the background.

I sit up, rubbing my eyes, willing myself to shake off the remnants of sleep. The orphanage had been harsh, but it had been full of life, noisy and chaotic. This house, however, feels like a museum, grand but devoid of any warmth. It's as if I'm merely a piece of art, meant to be seen but not touched, not understood. I feel like a ghost wandering through halls that don't belong to me.

And despite their smiles and polite words, the Whitmores don't see me either. I know they adopted me—like they adopted Theodore, Maxwell, and Julian—for the sake of appearances. We're just part of the decor, another set of trophies they can show off when the moment suits them. The boys seem fine with it. Maybe they're used to being invisible.

I, on the other hand, can't stop thinking about Valeria. She's like a wound that refuses to heal, an ever-present ache. The look on her face when I left Gloomwood behind is etched in my mind, as if branded there. The shock and hurt in her eyes, the betrayal when I was taken away...I didn't have a choice, but it doesn't stop me from wishing I had. I left her, and that guilt gnaws at me more than the quiet ever could.

Sliding out of bed, I let my feet sink into the plush carpet. Everything here is too perfect and delicate, but it only makes me feel more out of place. I can't help but sigh as I pull on a sweater. What's the point of all this luxury when it feels like a gilded cage? Even my adoptive brothers don't care about me, and I don't care about them. I've never been around boys before, so I avoid them as much as possible—except for the forced dinners or outings. They laugh, joke, and seem comfortable here, but I see through it. Beneath the surface, there's something off.

I drag myself downstairs for breakfast, already dreading the routine. Mr. Whitmore is seated at the head of the long dining table, hidden behind his newspaper, while Mrs. Whitmore talks quietly with the housekeeper. It's always the same stifling politeness, formal and distant.

They glance up as I enter.

"Camila," Mr. Whitmore says without much interest, gazing over the rim of his glasses. "We're having a party at the house this evening. I'm sending you and your brothers away for the night with Mrs. Deering. She'll look after you in the guest house."

I've only seen the guest house from a distance while wandering the estate. It's smaller, tucked away, hidden among the trees. Once, I saw the boys coming out of it. I've always wondered what goes on inside there, but I've never been curious enough to investigate. Now, I suppose, I'll finally find out.

I nod and take my usual seat at the table. Breakfast looks perfect as always—flawlessly arranged, the kind of meal you see in magazines—but I barely touch it. I can't stop thinking about Valeria. Without her, everything feels so pointless. She was my anchor, my tether to the world, and now, I'm floating aimlessly through life.

After our meal, I retreat to my room, pulling out my sketchbook. I lose myself in drawing like I always do, letting the familiar motion of my pencil on paper soothe me. Butterflies fill the pages. I can't help it—they remind me of her. We often used to talk about them, how free they were, how weightless. Drawing them makes me feel close to her, even though we're worlds apart now.

By the time evening arrives, I've sketched page after page of delicate wings and intricate patterns. Mrs. Deering knocks on my door, reminding me it's time to head to the guest house. I pack my things and toss my sketchbook into my bag, and as I sling it over my shoulder, I don't notice my pencil slipping to the floor.

Downstairs, the Whitmores are busy with preparations for the party. I pass through the foyer, catching fragments of their conversation with a woman scribbling notes. Mr. Whitmore's voice is low but sharp as he says something that sends a shiver through me.

"Make sure the basement is ready. And make sure no one goes down there, do you understand?"

I didn't even know this place had a basement. I shake off the uneasy feeling creeping up my spine. It's none of my business. Still, the way he said it sticks with me as Mrs. Deering leads us outside.

Dinner at the guest house is a quiet affair. The boys retreat to their rooms afterward while Mrs. Deering fusses over the dishes. I head to my temporary bedroom, unpacking my sketchbook and reaching for my pencil, only to realize it's missing. Groaning, I retrace my steps in my head, realizing I must've dropped it back at the mansion.

For a moment, I debate whether to sneak out and retrieve it. It seems risky, but I hate leaving things unfinished. If I hurry, no one will even notice I'm gone.

Slipping out the back door, I dart into the woods. The mansion looms ahead, imposing and dark. As I approach, something catches my eye—a man wearing a white mask, slipping out of a door I've never seen before.

Curiosity takes over and, instead of heading to the main entrance, I creep toward the mysterious door and slip inside just before it closes.

A narrow set of stairs spirals down into darkness, and I descend slowly, each step making my heart pound louder. At the bottom, I find myself in a room filled with monitors— dozens of screens showing different parts of the house. My stomach twists as I step closer, watching the guests mingling and drinking. Another screen grabs my attention—it features a large room with a stage in the middle, surrounded by chairs.

Masked figures drag a woman onto the stage, her body weak as she struggles. I gasp, my blood running cold as they tie her to a chair. *What the hell is this?*

I step back, panic seizing my chest. I need to help her. I race down the corridor and see double doors at the end of the hall.

That must be where she is. Without hesitation, I sprint toward them, flinging them open.

My body tenses when the masked man on the stage jerks the woman's head back by her hair. Her mouth falls open as she gasps for air, her eyes wide and glazed with terror. Blood drips down her face from the gash on her head. I can't breathe—I can't even blink. My heart hammers in my chest as I watch in horror, rooted to the spot. My legs scream at me to move, but I'm frozen, staring as the man pulls out a knife. He's going to kill her.

Do something!

Adrenaline surges through me, snapping me out of my stupor. I let out a strangled scream, rushing forward. "No! Stop!" I don't even know what I'm doing—I just know I can't watch this woman die. I charge toward the stage, but before I can reach him, someone grabs me from behind, yanking me back with brutal force. My body jerks and I thrash against the strong arms holding me. "Let me go!" I scream, kicking and twisting as hard as I can. The man's grip tightens, but I'm frantic.

The man on stage sneers at me from behind his mask, his hand still twisted in the woman's hair. She whimpers, her voice faint and broken. "No, please..." Her words are cut off as the knife presses to her throat.

My scream rips through the room as I throw my foot back with every ounce of strength I have, aiming for my captor's groin. I connect hard, and the man behind me grunts in pain, his grip loosening just enough for me to get away.

I stumble forward, dodging the hands reaching for me. Masked men close in on all sides, but I'm too fast. I duck under one man's arm and dart toward the door. My heart pounds in my ears as I push through, slamming it behind me.

Outside, the air is cool and sharp, and I gulp in a deep

breath, my chest heaving. I can't stop running. I hear footsteps behind me, heavy and fast. *They're coming.*

I break into a sprint, my feet pounding the ground as I race toward the trees. My lungs burn, my legs screaming with every step, but I don't dare look back. I just need to reach the woods, where I can disappear into the shadows and find a way out.

Out of nowhere, a force slams into my back, and I go flying, crashing into the ground hard. The impact knocks the wind out of me, and for a moment, I can't move. My face presses into the dirt, filling my mouth as I gasp for air.

Hands grip my shoulders, flipping me over. My head spins as I blink at the figure above me, my heart sinking into my stomach.

It's Mr. Whitmore.

He's not wearing a mask, but the cold, empty look in his eyes is worse than anything I could've imagined. He looks down at me, his lips curling into something like a smirk. "You shouldn't have seen that," he says, his voice calm—almost *too* calm.

I open my mouth to scream again, to beg, to say something, but before I can, I feel a sharp sting in my neck.

"No—" I gasp, but it's too late. The drug floods my veins, and my limbs go numb. My vision blurs as I struggle to keep my eyes open, but the darkness is too strong, pulling me under.

The last thing I hear is Mr. Whitmore's voice. "You never should've come here, Camila."

I WAKE UP TO BLINDING LIGHT, THE KIND THAT BURNS THROUGH my eyelids and makes me wince. Slowly, I force my eyes open, but the room around me swims in and out of focus.

Where am I?

I try to piece it together, but all I get is fragments. It's like someone ripped out entire chunks of my memory, leaving me hollow. My name...*What's my name*?

I look down at my body. My arms are tangled in tubes. IV lines snake out from my hands, pumping God knows what into my veins. My heart starts to hammer in my chest, my breathing coming in short, ragged bursts. Why am I hooked up to all this? Panic grips me like a vice.

"Hello?" My voice is hoarse, weak, like I haven't used it in days. I clear my throat and try again, louder this time. "Is anyone there?"

No response.

I struggle to sit up, tubes tugging at my skin, and the sharp pain that shoots through my arm makes me gasp. My head spins, but I grit my teeth and swing my legs over the side of the bed. The cool metal of the IV stand clinks as I move, sending my pulse racing.

I can't stay here. I don't know where *here* is, but something deep inside tells me I need to leave.

The moment I decide to act, my hands move on instinct, ripping the IVs out of my arms with a wince. Blood wells from the punctures, a small line running down my wrist, but I ignore it. I tear off the patches on my chest and the oxygen tube hooked to my nose, the beeping of the machines escalating into a sharp alarm.

I push myself off the bed and immediately collapse.

My legs give out from under me, a surge of dizziness overtaking my senses. I hit the cold floor hard, and pain explodes through my head as my skull feels like it's being split in two. I curl up, clutching my temples, trying to stop the world from spinning, nausea churning in my stomach.

I lie there for what feels like hours, every second dragging on, the pain searing through me. I don't know how long it takes, but eventually, the spinning stops enough for me to move. I force myself to sit up, bracing a hand against the floor, fighting to stay steady. My body feels all wrong, like I've been asleep forever, my muscles weak and brittle. How long have I been here?

I look around the room—no windows, no personal belongings, just sterile, cold surfaces. There's no file, no chart hanging from the bed, nothing that tells me who I am or what happened.

I crawl to the door, pulling myself up by the handle and carefully cracking it open. The hallway outside is long, stretching out into an unfamiliar maze of white walls. There's no sign of where I am.

I step out, but my body is sluggish, every movement slow and uncoordinated. I stumble forward, wincing as my bare feet hit the cold floor.

I hardly make it ten feet when I see two guards down the hall. They spot me, and panic hits like a freight train. I turn and run.

"Hey! Stop!" one of them shouts.

I don't look back. My legs are weak, barely holding me up, but I push through the burning in my lungs, the stabbing pain in my head. The air rushes against my face, my hospital gown flapping wildly as I bolt down the hallway.

I find a side door at the end of the corridor and slam through it, bursting outside into the open air. The cold hits me like a slap, my breath visible in the night.

I dash into the trees, the ground beneath me turning rough and uneven.

Branches whip at my face, sharp cuts opening on my skin as I weave through the forest. My heart pounds in my chest, echoing in my ears, but I don't slow down. I can't. The guards are still behind me, their shouts growing closer.

My feet are bare, every rock, every twig, digging into the soles, but the pain is nothing compared to the fear driving me forward. Then, I step on something sharp, and agony shoots through me. I scream, stumbling forward, my legs almost giving out, but I keep going.

I glance back as my foot catches on something—a root, maybe—and I fall. My body slams into the hard ground, my head cracking against a rock. Pain explodes behind my eyes, white-hot and searing.

I try to get up, to crawl, but my limbs refuse to obey. Darkness seeps into the edges of my vision, swallowing me whole as the guards' footsteps grow louder. They're close now, their voices just above me.

And then, everything goes black.

I WAKE TO THE SOUND OF RUSTLING LEAVES AND THE COLD BITE OF the ground beneath me.

My body feels heavy, weighed down by pain.

Slowly, I blink against the fog clouding my vision. The forest comes into focus—dark trees loom over me, their branches creaking as they sway in the night air.

I turn onto my back, wincing as a sharp pain stabs through my skull. The movement sends another wave of nausea rolling through me, and I clamp my eyes shut for a moment, trying to breathe through it. My head feels like it's splitting open, the dull throb now a searing ache, making it almost impossible to think.

When I finally open my eyes again, the moon stares back at me, huge and impossibly bright, hanging high above the trees. Its silver light cuts through the darkness. I wince, squinting against the glare drilling into my skull. It's beautiful, but it hurts. Everything hurts.

I try to move, to lift my arm, but my body is heavy, like I'm sinking into the ground. Every inch is a struggle.

My breath hitches as I reach up to touch my head. My fingers graze a large, wet gash near my forehead, and pain flares so violently, I can't stop the scream that rips from my throat. It echoes in the quiet of the forest, and I immediately regret it.

Shit.

I freeze, terror settling in. What if the guards heard me? What if they're still looking for me?

But the forest remains silent, save for the wind. No footsteps, no voices. No one comes for me.

I drop my hand and glance down at my fingers, blood smeared across my skin. Tears spring to my eyes, hot and stinging, and before I can stop them, they spill down my cheeks. Everything hurts so much. My body feels broken.

The pain, the fear, the exhaustion—they're all too much. I close my eyes, crying silently, and I wonder why the guards left me here in the first place. Why didn't they take me? Did they think I was already dead? Or maybe they just didn't care.

A small, fluttering movement catches my attention, and I slowly open my eyes. A monarch butterfly floats down from the dark sky, its orange-and-black wings illuminated by the moonlight. It's surreal, like something out of a dream. I watch, mesmerized, as it drifts closer, landing delicately on my knuckle, its wings fanning out, soft as silk against my skin.

For a moment, the world seems to still, and a strange, quiet peace washes over me. My breath steadies, the tears slowing.

I shut my lids again. This time, it's not out of pain, but something gentler.

For just a moment, I feel okay.

When I wake again, the world around me is softer. The sky is tinged with pale pinks and grays, the air cool and damp from the night. My head still throbs, though not as violently as before, and I can hear my own shallow breathing. The scent of pine and soil is sharp in the air, but something else cuts through it—a faint smell, like clean linen or soap.

I blink, and suddenly, I see someone.

A woman is hovering above me. My heart lurches, and instinctively, I try to move. Panic flares in my chest, and I let out a startled gasp. I struggle to push myself back, and the pain surges in response.

"Shh...it's okay. I'm not here to hurt you," she whispers, her voice calm. She reaches out and gently grabs my hand. "You're safe now. I'm just trying to help."

I want to believe her, but the fear is still there, tightening my throat. My body aches with every breath, the pounding in my head almost unbearable. I can't find the words to respond. All I can do is stare at her, wide-eyed, chest heaving, as my body trembles uncontrollably.

The woman shifts her weight, crouching down beside me. "Can you stand?" she asks, her grip firm as she helps lift me off the cold ground. I try to push myself up, but my legs feel like they're made of lead. She supports me, easing me to my feet. My head spins again, and I sway, nearly collapsing, but she holds me steady.

"I've got you," she says softly. Her touch is careful, her hands strong as they keep me from falling again.

I'm barely on my feet when she reaches into her bag and pulls out a small syringe. The moment I see it, panic rips through me. My heart kicks into overdrive, and I thrash, shoving her away with what little strength I have.

"No! Don't!" I cry, my voice coming out raw and broken.

She grabs my arm. "It's just to help. I promise." Her voice

remains calm, though more urgent now. "This is just pain medication. You're hurt, and I need to treat you, okay?"

I keep struggling, my breath ragged, but my body's giving out. I'm too weak, and my mind is screaming in every direction. Still, something in her voice makes me want to trust her.

She meets my eyes. "I'm Rachel. I'm part of a group that rescues women in danger. I'm on your side, I swear."

I hesitate, but what do I have to lose at this point? I'm too exhausted to fight anymore. I relax just enough for her to pierce me with the needle. The sharp prick stings, but it's nothing compared to everything else.

"Good," Rachel murmurs as she finishes. "It's going to help with your injuries. You probably have a concussion, but this should dull the worst of it."

I wait, not sure what to expect, but after a few minutes, a warm numbness starts spreading through my limbs. The sharp edge of pain in my head dulls, just enough for me to breathe again without wanting to scream. I feel strong enough to stand on my own.

Rachel slips an arm around my waist, supporting my weight as we start walking. My legs are still shaky, and I lean heavily on her, but it feels good to move again, even if every step makes me dizzy. The trees thin out ahead, and I catch glimpses of an open road, an old truck parked nearby.

"How old are you?" Rachel asks, her voice soft as she guides me forward. "What's your name?"

I open my mouth to answer, but the words don't come. Instead, a knot tightens in my chest. "I...I don't remember," I finally manage. "I don't know who I am. I only remember waking up in a room, and..." I hesitate, the memory flooding back, bringing fear with it. "Two men. They were chasing me."

Rachel's face darkens. "Two men?" Her grip tightens slightly on my arm. "We'll take care of it. You won't have to worry about them anymore, I promise."

As we walk, Rachel glances down at my wrist. "What's this?" she murmurs, lifting my arm gently.

I look down, too disoriented to have noticed it before: a bracelet—a hospital band, maybe—wrapped tightly around my wrist. It's blank, except for a single date printed on it: November 3, 1998.

Rachel studies it for a moment. "That must be your birthday," she says quietly. "It's all we've got to go on for now."

My birthday. It doesn't feel like much, but it's something, a small piece of the puzzle.

We step out of the forest, the sunlight breaking over the horizon in soft rays. The truck looms ahead, an old beat-up vehicle with dust coating its sides. Rachel helps me to the back seat, where two other young women wait. They immediately reach out, helping me get comfortable.

"Welcome to Solace," Rachel says softly as she closes the door behind me.

A FEW MONTHS LATER, SOLACE HAS BECOME MY HOME. AFTER finding me almost dead in the forest, Rachel brought me to the underground headquarters. The physical wounds healed quickly, but my head took longer. The concussion was bad, and I spent weeks with my brain wrapped in fog, my thoughts stumbling over themselves as I tried to piece together fragments of a life I didn't even remember.

But now, I'm whole again—physically, at least. I don't get dizzy anymore, and the headaches are gone. But despite all the healing, I still can't remember. I don't know who I was before waking up in that sterile room with those men chasing me. No matter how hard I try to push through the haze, nothing comes.

I don't know my real name. I don't remember where I grew

up, what my family was like. I can't even remember what the men who were after me looked like. Their faces are shadows in the back of my mind, blurry and unrecognizable.

Sometimes, I wonder if I ever mattered to anyone. It has been months since I escaped that place, and there hasn't been a single missing person report or news article mentioning me. No searches, no flyers, no pleas for help from a frantic family. Nothing. Whoever I was before, it seems like no one's looking for her.

Part of me wonders if I ever had a family at all. Maybe I didn't. Maybe I was just another lost girl no one cared about. Or worse—maybe whoever they were wanted to get rid of me, and they succeeded. I'm gone.

So, I gave myself a new name. It started when Rachel asked what I wanted to be called, and I had nothing. No memories, no identity, just this empty space where a person was supposed to be. I named myself after something I'd always loved: horror films. They're a comfort somehow, even in the middle of this nightmare I'm living in. I don't remember anything about my past, but I do remember loving the movie *Verónica*.

So, I became Ronnie.

UNSOLVED

15

Valeria

Verónica's words hit me like a sledgehammer.

My heart stops, and it feels like I'm suddenly outside my own body, watching this moment unfold from a distance. *No.* No, it can't be. I try to speak, but nothing comes out. My throat is tight, my mouth dry. I feel the blood drain from my face, leaving me cold.

"Camila?" I finally manage to croak. "That's not possible."

But as I say the words, something inside me shifts, like a piece of a puzzle finally sliding into place. The way she moves, the way she talks, the way she always seems to know just a little too much—I'd felt it from the start. That familiarity tugged at me, like an old memory buried deep. I was drawn to her, even when it didn't make sense. I just couldn't figure out why—until now. My head spins as I grab the edge of the table to steady myself.

"I didn't remember," Ronnie—no, *Camila*—says, her voice soft. "Not until I saw the tattoo. Then, it all came back. The Whitmores taking me away. My name. I didn't know who I was for so long, but I'm her, Valeria."

I stare at her, my heart breaking and mending all at once.

"This can't be real." My voice cracks, tears welling in my eyes. I shake my head, trying to fight them back, but they spill over anyway. "You're not her. You can't be her. She's dead."

"They wanted everyone to believe that," Camila—*Ronnie*—says, her voice tight. She leans forward, desperation in her eyes, pleading with me to believe her. "But I survived. They might've erased who I was, but they couldn't break me. *Camila* might be dead, but I—Verónica—am very much alive."

My vision blurs, and I press my palms to my temples, trying to wrap my mind around this as my body trembles with disbelief. How can this be real? All these years of searching, of mourning, of thinking she was gone, and now, she's here, sitting across from me.

"I looked for you," I whisper, the tears choking me now. "I never stopped looking for you."

She reaches for my hand, and I don't pull away. The moment her fingers touch mine, I feel it—something I'd lost so long ago. A warmth spreads through me, even though I'm still shaking.

"I'm here now," she says, her voice barely audible, but it hits me like a tidal wave. "I'm here, Valeria."

A sob escapes my throat, and I throw myself at her, wrapping my arms around her neck like I'll never let go. She's real. She's here. After all this time, after all the pain, she's back. She remembers.

We hold each other, and I can't stop crying. It's everything I've been dreaming of, everything I thought I'd never get.

"What did they do to you?" I manage to ask between ragged breaths, my face buried in her shoulder.

"They must've drugged me enough to cause a memory lapse," she says, her voice shaking now too. "I don't remember everything, but they messed with my head. I didn't know who I was for years. I became someone else. But your tattoo brought me back. It made me remember."

I pull back to look at her, wiping my tears with the back of my hand. "I can't believe this. I thought I lost you forever."

Ronnie smiles, but it's sad, full of everything we've been through. "I thought I was gone too, but I found my way back. I found my way to you."

Everything clicks—the strange feeling I had the first time we met, the inexplicable pull toward her, even when I didn't know why. I knew her, on some deep, instinctual level, even if I couldn't explain it.

"The necklace," I mutter.

Ronnie lets out a sigh. "It was the only belonging I had when I left that place. I didn't know where it came from or what it even meant, but I kept it all these years. Now, I know I was wearing it for you. I missed you every fucking day after I was taken from Gloomwood."

I reach for Ronnie's face, cupping her cheeks. Her skin is warm under my fingertips, and I can feel her breath hitch as I pull her closer.

"Camila," I whisper, her name like a prayer on my lips.

She doesn't say anything. She just looks at me with those same eyes that have always known me—*truly known me*—even before all this.

My gaze wanders over her face, taking her in the way I should've done from the very start. Ronnie has changed so much, but now, with everything out in the open, I can see the thread that connects the girl I once knew to the woman in front of me.

Back then, she had long, wild blonde curls tumbling past her shoulders in unruly waves. I remember how they framed her face, making her seem ethereal. She was beautiful then, so beautiful that it almost hurt to look at her sometimes.

Now, she's different. Short, black curls cling close to her neck, the sharpness of her new look matching the edge she has grown into. Her features, once soft, are now bold. Tattoos snake up her arms and across her collarbone, intricate designs that tell stories I don't yet know.

But somehow, she's just as stunning—*more* stunning. The woman in front of me is fierce, powerful, owning every inch of who she is. The changes don't hide her beauty; they amplify it. There's a rawness to her now, a danger that wasn't there before, but it's beautiful. *She's* beautiful.

I reach out, tracing the ink on her arm. "You've changed," I murmur, not as an accusation but as an acknowledgment.

She gives me a half-smile, one corner of her mouth tugging up. "We both have," she says softly, her hand covering mine, pressing my palm to her tattooed skin. "But you know what? I think you were there with every version of me, guiding me back. I couldn't be who I am now without you."

Her words send a shiver down my spine, and I feel that same familiar pull, stronger now than ever. She's right. No matter how much has changed, she's still Camila. She's still *mine*. I'm still hers.

Her gaze flicks down to my mouth, and suddenly, the air between us is thick and charged. I don't even think about it; I lean in, crashing my lips against hers.

The second we touch, everything inside me ignites. Her lips are soft but urgent, moving against mine in a way that makes my entire body hum with energy. I can't stop. I don't *want* to stop. I've been waiting for this moment for so long, and now that it's here, I'm terrified to let it slip away.

I pull her closer, my fingers tangling in her hair, and she responds just as fiercely, her hands gripping my waist as she kisses me harder, deeper. It's like we're trying to make up for all the lost time, for every second we didn't know each other, every moment we were apart. I can feel her wild heartbeat against my chest, matching mine.

The kiss turns desperate, needy. My fingers glide down her neck, across her shoulders, and I feel her hands slipping under my shirt. Her touch sends shivers down my spine, and I can't get enough of it. I need more.

I let out a gasp as she pulls me onto her lap, her hands exploring my body like it's the first time, but also like she has always known exactly where to touch, exactly how to make me come alive. My skin is burning, and all I can think about is how much I've missed her, how much I want her right now.

We break the kiss for a moment, panting, our foreheads pressed together, but the moment is short-lived. Ronnie's fingers are already at the hem of my shirt, tugging it up. I help her, lifting it over my head, and then her hands are on me again, skin on skin, and it's *electric*.

"Valeria," she groans.

The look in her eyes says everything. She wants this badly too. She pulls me closer, her lips finding mine again, and suddenly, our hands are everywhere—on skin, in hair, tugging and ripping at the fabric between us as if it's the only thing keeping us from each other.

I slide my hands under her shirt, cupping her breasts, and they feel perfect in my hands. She gasps against my lips as I pull on her nipple.

Ronnie's lips trace a slow path down my jawline, and when she reaches my neck, her teeth sink in sharply. I gasp, a mix of pain and pleasure sparking through me, but before I can protest, her tongue glides over the mark, soothing the sting and sending shivers across my skin. Her kisses trail lower, across my collarbone, down my chest. When her mouth closes over my breast, a jolt of electricity shoots straight to my core, leaving me breathless.

"I need you. Now," I whisper, my hands fumbling clumsily with the buttons on her pants.

Clothes fall to the floor in a tangled mess, and Ronnie pulls me onto the bed, her body pressing into mine.

"God, Valeria," she breathes, her voice thick with desire.

"How could I have ever forgotten you? You're perfect. Everything I've ever needed. Just like this. Bare. Under me. Completely mine."

She straddles me, her thigh pressing between my legs as she lowers herself just enough to kiss my nipples, teasing me with the soft scrape of her teeth. Her hips begin to move, grinding her slick center against my leg, and the feel of her arousal against my skin sends my own need spiraling.

"Please, Ronnie," I whine, arching beneath her. "Let me taste you. I've been dying for it since you made me come in the hallway. Please."

Without a word, Ronnie moves, positioning herself above me, her knees framing my head as she grants me exactly what I've been begging for.

My tongue flicks against her, and she lets out a loud, throaty moan. God, she tastes like heaven—sweet and intoxicating. I grip her thighs and pull her down onto my mouth, pressing her against me so she's no longer hovering. With her fully seated on my lips, I suck her clit into my mouth, swirling my tongue with just the right pressure. Ronnie's hips begin to rock forward, riding my tongue as I work her closer to the edge.

"Oh my God, Val. Princesa," she breathes, her voice thick with lust. "Não pares." *Don't stop.*

I slip a hand between her legs from behind, teasing her entrance with my fingers. She gasps, a breathy mewl escaping her as I slide two fingers inside her. "Come for me," I murmur against her skin. "Make a mess of my face."

I'm so turned on, I can't resist. My other hand slips between my own legs, fingers finding my clit. I spread my thighs wide and gather some of my own wetness, circling the sensitive nub with just the right touch. It feels so good, I can't help but moan against Ronnie's pussy, the vibrations sending her even higher.

Hearing me pleasure myself drives her wild, and her hips move faster, grinding her center over my mouth, her moans growing louder, more desperate. She's so close, teetering right on the edge.

"Ah! Fuck, Valeria, I'm coming," she gasps, her body trembling as she finally lets go. Her legs shake, struggling to keep her steady as she falls apart, screaming my name.

Once Ronnie catches her breath, she leans down and kisses me fiercely. The taste of her still lingers on my lips, mingling with the sweetness of her tongue, making me crave more.

Her hands grip my shoulders as she suddenly flips me over, positioning me on top of her, straddling her hips. "Grab my belt," she commands. Confused but eager to please, I pick it off the floor and hand it to her.

"Come closer." I lower myself toward her, and she loops the strap around my neck, pulling it snug. My breath hitches, a tightness forming in my throat as I struggle for air. Ronnie holds the belt like a leash, a wicked smirk tugging at the corner of her lips.

"Ride me, princesa," she orders, her voice dark with desire. "Put your soaking cunt on mine and make me come again." She grabs my still-wet fingers, pulling them into her mouth, slowly sucking and licking them clean. "Use me to get off. Show me what a good little slut you are."

Her words send a wave of heat crashing through me. I don't think I could be any more turned on.

I lower myself between her legs, positioning my hips so my center rests perfectly against hers. Gripping her knee for leverage, I begin rolling my hips, the friction coaxing a deep moan from my throat as I grind down, her clit rubbing against mine in a delicious rhythm.

I close my eyes, letting the sensation wash over me, until I feel the sharp tug of leather around my neck. It tightens, choking me, cutting off my air. "Eyes open, butterfly," Ronnie says, her voice commanding. "I want to see them roll back when you come for me, as I steal all the air you breathe."

I lock eyes with her as I move, desperate to find my release. Our wetness mixes, slick and hot, and I can hear her inhales coming in ragged gasps, spot her chest rising and falling rapidly beneath me.

"Fuck, fuck, fuck," I whimper, the orgasm rising, creeping closer with every grind of our bodies.

Ronnie wraps the belt tighter, the pressure increasing around my throat, making it harder to breathe. My vision blurs and my chest heaves, but the lack of air only sharpens the pleasure. I'm dizzy, on the verge of passing out, and when I come, harder than I think I ever have, my body threatens to give out.

"Yes, princesa. Just like that."

I ride out the last of my orgasm until Ronnie tenses beneath me, her climax overtaking her.

I bend down to kiss her, and she pulls back just enough to look into my eyes.

She brushes a strand of hair from my face, her fingers tracing the curve of my jaw. Her breath is warm against my skin, and for a second, the world feels impossibly still.

"You did so fucking well, butterfly."

My cheeks feel hot at her praise, and I smile shyly. "Thank you."

"Do you feel it?" Ronnie says. "It's like the stars waited for us—like every scar, every broken piece, was leading us to this point."

I blink, the intensity of her words sinking deep into my chest. My heart pounds as she goes on, her fingers moving to trace the tattoo on my rib, the one that sparked this entire moment.

"*Mors tua, vita mea*," she murmurs, her eyes burning into mine. "*Your death, my life*. But it was never about death, was it? It was always life. *You* gave me life, Valeria. Even when they tried to take it from me, I held on because somewhere, deep down, I knew you were out there, waiting for me."

Tears prick at my eyes, but I can't look away from her. She's everything—my past, my present, my future—all in one. And she's right; we've been waiting for this, maybe even longer than we realized.

"And I'm not lost anymore. I'm not broken. We found each other, and nothing—*nothing*—can tear us apart again."

16

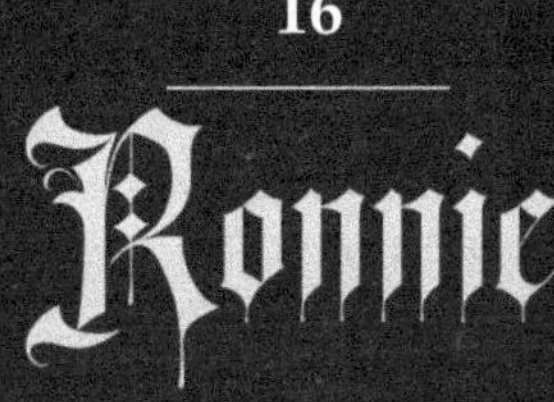Ronnie

I'm still coming down from my high, my breath steadying as I watch Valeria catch hers. Her body, still glowing, lies beside me, and for a moment, everything feels right. *Finally.*

I glance down at the mess we've made, and a smile tugs at the corner of my lips. But then, I notice the blood, our clothes still damp and stained from earlier. I should clean her up.

I remove the belt from around her neck, rubbing at her red skin to soothe the soreness.

When I'm satisfied, I get up slowly, legs wobbly, and move to the small drawer near the bed, rifling through it, trying to find anything useful. My fingers brush against some old rags. *Perfect.* I grab one and head to the adjoining bathroom.

The water runs cold as I wet the cloth, squeezing out just enough water before heading back to her. She's still lying there, her eyes closed, but I can tell she's not asleep. "Hey," I whisper, kneeling beside her. "Deixa-me tomar conta de ti." *Let me take care of you.*

She looks into my eyes, seeing the sincerity there. "Why?"

"Because you're mine now."

I begin to gently wipe the blood off her skin, working my

way over her arms, down her stomach. There's a softness in my movements, but underneath it all, I can't believe it's real. What's shocking is that I remember everything—every detail I buried, every connection I missed. All this time, it wasn't just about the Whitmores.

When I'm done cleaning her up, I help her slip her shirt back on, the fabric sticking slightly to her skin where the blood splattered. The red stains contrast deeply with her skin, but it doesn't make her any less beautiful. If anything, it makes her look stronger.

I stand, grabbing my own clothes from the floor and tugging them on, piece by piece. My body aches from the fight, but my mind is sharper than it has ever been.

She watches me as I dress, her brow furrowing slightly. "So, what's the plan?"

I pull my shirt over my head and sit beside her, leaning in close enough to feel her warmth again. "We go after them—on *our* terms this time. And we make sure they never hurt anyone again. There's no way we let those motherfuckers tear us down."

Her lips curl into a determined smile. "I'm ready."

We spend the next few minutes devising a plan of action and decide to leave the security of my old bedroom. This room is tucked away in an area of the mansion off-limits to everyone but the family, which explains why no one has come looking for us yet. Eventually, though, they'll realize we're not just hiding and come for us.

But instead of fleeing or finding another place to hide, we're going to find *them* and teach them a lesson they'll never forget. We've had enough of the Whitmores thinking they can own us, control us, and do whatever they please.

When we've finally gathered ourselves, we slip out of the bedroom quietly, Valeria close behind me. Our footsteps are barely audible as we move down the dim hallway. We have my knife and her kubotan, but we need better weapons if we're going to succeed.

As we make our way down the corridor, the memories drift back to me, the architecture of the mansion triggering old thoughts. "I remember this hallway," I murmur. The walls look familiar, the faded patterns of the wallpaper. "There are swords on one of these walls, I'm sure of it."

We keep walking until the passage splits in two directions. "This way." I lead her to the right, my instincts kicking in—and there they are, hanging on the wall like artifacts, just as I remembered.

"Bingo." I take two down, handing one to Valeria. She holds it like she was born for this, the steel glinting as she swings it over her shoulder. The fierce determination in her eyes is intoxicating.

"Fuck, Val," I groan quietly. "It's taking everything in me not to shove the handle of that sword up your sweet cunt right now."

Valeria grins, that familiar fire in her gaze. "Another time," she teases, her voice a sultry whisper that makes my pulse race.

But now is not the time for distractions. We reach the end of the second floor and find the stairwell.

"I know exactly where they'll be."

"In the basement?" Valeria asks, her voice tense.

I nod. "Yeah, where we first met. They'll be down there, performing that ritual." The thought of it makes my skin crawl, the memory of that room flickering through my mind.

Valeria shivers beside me, but she grips the sword tighter. "We'll barge in and stop them. No more sacrifices, no more hiding. We'll end this."

When we reach the basement, Valeria whistles softly beside me. "These monitors are just as creepy as they were the first time."

"Yeah," I agree. "When I followed you down here, the space

felt oddly familiar. I figured it was just because I spend so much time in front of screens."

Valeria's brow furrows. "Oh, right. When you spent hours *stalking* me?" She moves past me, but I grab a handful of her hair, pulling her body flush against mine as she hisses from the strain.

"Yes, *stalking* you. You might see it as an invasion of privacy, but deep down, I know you get a twisted thrill knowing someone had eyes on you, especially when you were alone, humping your pillows like a filthy fucking girl." I tug harder on her hair. "I'll never stop watching you, butterfly. Not in this lifetime."

She gasps as I release her, and I savor the distress in her eyes.

"You're a psychopath," she says, but I just laugh.

"The room is down this hall," I say, pointing ahead. "We'll have to be quiet to avoid drawing attention."

"Wait. What about Isabel?" Valeria asks, stopping abruptly and pulling out her phone. "Still nothing," she says, showing me the screen.

"Let's check the cameras. If she's still in the house, she'll show up on one of these monitors."

We return to the screens and scan each feed, but Isabel doesn't appear. The images change rapidly, and still, she's nowhere to be seen.

"They must've taken her out of the mansion," I speculate. Then, it hits me. "She's at the guest house."

Valeria looks at me, confused.

I realize I had forgotten about my three adoptive brothers: Theodore, Maxwell, and Julian. "They probably took her to the house beyond the forest. We'll find her once we're done here."

Valeria agrees, and we head back to the double doors. I glance back at her. "Are you ready?"

"Yes," she replies, her voice steady.

I crack them open and hear the faint murmur of a male voice chanting.

"From darkened depths and sacred fire, we offer blood in deep desire. Spirits heed and grant us grace as we unveil this sacred place."

A shiver runs down my spine, and Valeria's eyes widen in alarm.

We slip into the room quietly. Thankfully, no one notices us, their attention fixed on the ritual.

"By this rite, our will is cast. Through night and flame, our bond shall last," the man continues.

I lean in close to Valeria's ear. "Are you sure you're okay with this, butterfly? If it's too much—" She cuts me off.

"No. I need to do this. I'll be fine, I promise."

I nod and signal for Valeria to go left while I take the right. We part ways, moving stealthily toward the group. The man at the altar has his back to us, chanting to something or someone.

"Guide us with your unseen hand as we fulfill this fated stand."

I grab one of the men from behind, wrapping my arm around his mouth to muffle his cries and stab him in the neck with my knife. Valeria sneaks up on another, slicing his throat with the sword before he even has a chance to react.

We continue moving through the room, taking down the masked men one by one, our swords glistening with their blood.

But as the main man completes his chant, someone turns and spots us.

"Intruders!" he shouts.

I give Valeria a look, and we both know it's time to run. We sprint out of the room, as the remaining men chase us, their weapons clanging as they scramble to catch up.

"We need to split up," I shout over my shoulder to Valeria. "It's the only way we'll make it out."

Valeria nods. "Be careful."

I run down a narrow corridor, my breath coming in ragged gasps. My mind races with potential escape routes, but every door seems locked or blocked.

Meanwhile, I watch Valeria from across the hall, darting through the mansion's maze-like interior and slipping behind a grand mantle. Her hiding spot seems safe, but when I look around, I spot a man approaching her from behind.

My eyes widen in horror as I realize what's about to happen.

I scan the room for anything I can use to help Valeria. My gaze lands on another man standing a few feet away, his weapon drawn, oblivious to the imminent danger behind him. Quietly, I sneak up on him, my sword gripped tightly. With a swift movement, I strike him in the head, the blade slicing through flesh and bone with a sickening crunch. The man crumples to the floor, and I quickly grab his gun.

I aim the weapon at the man approaching Valeria, and with a steady hand, I fire. The shot rings out, echoing through the mansion, and the man falls, a neat hole appearing in his temple. He drops forward, collapsing inches from Valeria.

She catches sight of the fallen man and muffles a scream, her eyes wide with shock. She scrambles to her feet, moving out of the way as I rush to her side.

"Are you okay?"

Tears spring in her eyes as she nods. "Yes."

Seconds later, someone clears their throat. We turn toward the sound to find Mr. Whitmore standing at the living room entrance, his presence as imposing as ever. His gaze shifts to Valeria first. "Well, well, well, what do we have here? One of our guests causing a ruckus in my home?"

Valeria stands tall, her voice unwavering as she challenges him. "Stay away from us. We're not here to play games."

Mr. Whitmore laughs, a sinister sound that sends a chill

down my spine. "Oh, you think you can just waltz in here and threaten me? How amusing."

I step forward, feeling a surge of anger. "You haven't changed one bit, *Lionel*," I say, my voice filled with disgust.

Mr. Whitmore's confusion turns to recognition as he focuses on me. "Camila? I thought you were dead."

I meet his gaze with a cold stare. "That's what you wanted to believe. Unfortunately for you, your men didn't think to check if I was still breathing."

His eyes narrow. "You should have stayed dead."

Valeria steps in front of me, her sword ready. "We're not here to argue. We're here to stop you."

Mr. Whitmore's smile fades, replaced by a grim expression. "You're too late. The ritual is nearly complete, and nothing you do can change that."

I take a deep breath, feeling the weight of his words. "We're not leaving until you pay for what you've done."

His eyes flash with a threat. "You think you can take me down? I have more power than you can imagine."

I tighten my grip on the gun I'd hidden behind my back.

Mr. Whitmore's gaze shifts to the remaining men in the room, and his voice turns cold and commanding. "Deal with them," he orders, pointing at us. "Make sure they don't interfere."

The men begin to move, and Valeria and I brace ourselves for the fight.

As they move on us, I scan the room desperately for anything that could give us an advantage. My eyes land on a canister of gas used to light the fireplace, next to it, a box of matches. It's our only chance. I quickly turn to Valeria, urgency in my voice.

"Valeria, get that canister."

Valeria doesn't hesitate. She darts toward it as I keep my

gun trained on Mr. Whitmore, trying to maintain a steady aim. His menacing laughter fills the room.

"If you shoot me," he taunts, "my men won't hesitate to take you down. Proceed carefully, *Camila*."

His words send a burst of rage through me, and I almost growl out my response. "It's Verónica now, you piece of shit."

His expression falters slightly, but his arrogance remains. "Ah, *Verónica*. How quaint, though it changes nothing. You're still outnumbered and outmatched."

Valeria returns with the canister. I give her a nod, my grip on the gun strong, and whisper, "On three, throw the canister into the fireplace." I reach for the matches. "One, two, three."

Valeria throws the fuel just as I fire at Whitmore's men, hitting them in the knees. One by one, they collapse to the floor. My adoptive father scrambles for a gun, but he's too slow. Valeria charges at him, sending him sprawling. As he hits the carpet, she raises her sword and drives it through his chest, his dying gurgles echoing through the room.

I strike a match and prepare to toss it into the fireplace. Valeria sees what I'm doing and moves to exit the living room.

I throw the match, and we both sprint away.

UNSOLVED

17

Valeria

We push through the main doors, and just as we hit the grand staircase outside, a deafening explosion rocks the air. I drop to my knees, instinctively shielding my face with my arms.

The heat slams into us like a wall, and I can barely make out the towering flames now consuming the mansion.

Ronnie pulls me up, and we stumble down the marble stairs, my legs shaky from the adrenaline and the sheer magnitude of what just happened. I feel a sharp pain in my side where a piece of debris must have struck me, but I barely register it over the rush of relief.

At the bottom of the steps, we collapse, sitting on the cold stone, panting heavily. The mansion behind us is an inferno now, a fiery beacon against the dark sky. The flames roar and crackle, and the heat is intense, but it feels strangely comforting.

I glance at Ronnie, whose face is smeared with soot and blood, a wild look in her eyes. She breaks into a shaky laugh, and I can't help but join her. The laughter comes out as hysteria, the kind you only have when you've just come out of a nightmare.

Ronnie fumbles in her pocket, pulling out a pack of cigarettes. She waves it in front of me with a triumphant grin. "Smoke?" she offers.

I manage a tired smile, reaching into my own pocket for the box of matches. I hold it up, wiggling it between my fingers. "I grabbed these before the place started burning, just in case."

Ronnie takes a cigarette from the pack, holding it out to me. I accept it, and she lights it. After the tip catches fire, she sparks her own, and we both inhale deeply.

"Hell of a way to end the night," I say, taking a long drag. Ronnie laughs in response.

I chuckle, shaking my head. "I can't believe we actually did it, Camila—*Ronnie*," I correct myself. "I found you. And all those women...No more."

Ronnie nods, her expression softening. "It's over, and I'm not going anywhere this time." Her face morphs into something with a hint of amusement. "Remember when you thought you were just going to sneak in, grab some info, and leave?"

I laugh, despite the pain in my side. "Yeah, I remember. That was before we blew the place up and had to run for our lives."

"Quite the twist," Ronnie says, a smirk now playing on her lips. "But look at us. It feels almost poetic."

I lean back against the stone steps, feeling the heat on my skin. "Poetic and a bit absurd."

Ronnie takes another drag from her cigarette, the embers glowing brightly in the darkness. "Guess we're the last ones standing, huh, butterfly? *Mors tua, vita mea.*"

I smile, leaning forward to capture Verónica's lips in a searing kiss.

"*Mors tua, vita mea.*"

Epilogue

RONNIE

I sit in my office, the familiar sound of computers filling the silence. It has become a ritual, watching Valeria as she starts her day. The whole mess with the Whitmores may be behind us—*sort of*—but it hasn't dulled my need to see her every second I can.

The monitors flicker to life, and there she is, stepping out of her bedroom, wearing nothing but panties and a paper-thin tank top. Her nipples press against the fabric, hair still damp, clinging to her skin like dewdrops on a petal. My pulse quickens. God, she's stunning.

Months have passed since that grim night at the estate, and we've been inseparable ever since. Years apart melted away as if they'd never existed, but it's still not enough. I crave her presence, day and night. I've been begging her to move in with me for weeks, and finally, she gave in.

As Valeria moves through the kitchen, a sense of calm washes over me. She's not working today—it's Saturday—but nothing changes her morning routine. I lean back in my seat, taking a sip of my own drink, knowing I'll see her soon to help pack up her things. Still, even that anticipation can't quell the urge to see her now.

She pauses mid-step, glancing upward, her gaze locking onto the camera nestled atop the cabinets. A wicked grin spreads across her face, eyes gleaming. Slowly, her arm rises, and she flips me off, her grin turning into a devilish smirk. My breath catches.

The memory of the night we came back to her place after burning down the Whitmore estate flashes vividly through my head.

The wind rushed past us as we rode my motorcycle, Valeria behind me with her arms wrapped tightly around my waist. I could feel the warmth of her body pressed against my back, her legs snug against mine. Her skirt had ridden up her thighs, exposing smooth skin that brushed against me each time I shifted gears or leaned into a turn. Every time she tightened her hold, a jolt of electricity crackled between us. My heart raced faster, and I couldn't help but smile beneath my helmet. We're finally back together.

When we arrived at Valeria's building, I slowed the bike, steering it into a parking spot. The engine's roar faded into a gentle purr before I cut it off.

Valeria's grip loosened, but she didn't let go immediately.

When I turned my head, our eyes met as she lifted her helmet. Despite the soot smeared across her face and the streaks of crimson staining her skin and clothes, she was a goddess—her hair a light, wavy cascade, her eyes fierce and alive. The contrast of the grime and blood only seemed to heighten her beauty, making her seem otherworldly, untouchable. Even in her disheveled state, she was breathtaking.

"How do you know where I live?" she asked with a little bite in her tone, cutting through the silence.

Valeria caught my mischievous smirk.

"You know what? Never mind," she said, rolling her eyes.

When we reached her door, I stepped in behind her. The air carried the faint scent of her perfume, and it made my insides fucking tingle.

I glanced back at Valeria, who stared at me with confusion.

Ignoring her questioning look, I walked into the kitchen and began to open cabinets, searching through them for pots and pans, my hands moving almost automatically as I gathered ingredients from the fridge and pantry.

"What are you doing?" Valeria asked.

"You have to eat," I replied casually.

Her gaze flickered between me and the stuff in my hands.

"How do you even know your way around my kitchen?"

I paused briefly, a playful smile spreading across my face as I looked up at the corner of the kitchen ceiling. "Say cheese," I quipped.

Valeria stood, dumbfounded as I pointed out where each camera was.

She couldn't even find it in herself to be mad at me for the stalking anymore, and didn't ask me to take them down. Not like I would've given her the option anyway.

I come back to reality, bringing my attention to the screens in front of me.

Valeria hops onto the counter, legs spread as she leans back. My heart stutters.

Holy shit.

Her fingers slip under the band of her panties, sliding them aside to reveal her wet, glistening folds. A low groan escapes my throat as I sink deeper into my leather chair. My hand drifts to my chest, squeezing one breast before I pinch my nipple, sending a shockwave through me.

Valeria's eyes stay fixed on the camera, her fingers tracing over her slick slit, spreading her wetness with deliberate slowness. My mouth waters when she plunges two fingers deep into herself, her head tipping back, lips parting in a silent moan. I curse the lack of audio, desperate to hear her gasps of pleasure.

Her movements quicken, fingers pumping furiously while

her other hand circles her clit. I mirror her, slipping my hand down, finding my clit already swollen and aching. Electricity buzzes under my skin and my eyes flutter, but I force them open. Valeria's putting on a show, just for me. My perfect butterfly.

Her chest rises and falls, body trembling as her climax approaches. I want to be there. I *should* be there, making her come with my own hands. My pleasure builds alongside hers, my heart racing, skipping, then racing again.

Valeria's body tenses, legs shaking as she comes, *hard*. I watch, captivated, as her orgasm crashes over her. She leans back, eyes glazed, lips curved into a satisfied smirk. She pulls her panties back in place, hops off the counter, and resumes making her coffee, as if she hadn't just wrecked me through the screen.

Fuck this. I'm going over there.

I shove my chair back, fastening my pants as I rush from the office. Fifteen minutes later, I'm off my motorcycle and bolting up to her apartment.

The door's unlocked, just as I hoped. My filthy girl left it open for me.

I burst inside, searching for her. I find her lounging on the couch, sipping her coffee like nothing happened. She doesn't flinch as I approach, and I don't say a word.

Dropping to my knees, I grab her waist, pulling her to the edge of the couch. I tear her soaked panties off, breathing in her intoxicating scent before tucking them into my pocket. Her pussy is bare and beautiful, and I waste no time diving in.

Her taste invades my senses as I moan against her skin. "Valeria," I murmur. "Butterfly. You're going to kill me with this perfect cunt."

She reclines back, getting comfortable while I devour her like she's the only thing I'll ever need. Nothing compares to the taste of her. I flick my tongue in tight circles over her clit, applying just enough pressure to make her body writhe. Her moans come faster now, filling the room.

Spitting onto my hand, I slide two fingers deep inside her, curling them to hit that perfect spot. "Fuck, yes," Valeria cries, her voice a breathless plea. "Right there. Don't stop."

Her arousal soaks my hand, dripping down onto the couch. I press my thumb into her tight asshole, feeling the muscle squeeze around me. I'm so close to losing control; my need to touch myself is nearly overwhelming, but Valeria's pussy is greedy, and I'm more than happy to let her take everything I have.

Her body locks up, a scream tearing from her throat as she comes, squirting all over my hand. I slip my fingers out, giving her space to ride the waves of her orgasm. Cum splashes across me, and I return my mouth to her, savoring the last drops of her climax.

Her entire body trembles, breathless and spent. "Holy fuck," she pants, a shy smile tugging at her lips. "I made a mess."

I chuckle, wiping my chin. "You sure did, princesa. Let me clean you up."

I move in again, but Valeria claps her legs shut with a giggle. "No, no. I can't take any more." Her laughter is soft and sweet, sending warmth through me. I get lost in her eyes, overwhelmed by how deeply I love this woman.

"What?" she asks, her voice curious, pulling me from my trance.

"I just love you," I say, leaning in to kiss her, soft and slow. "You're the air I need to survive, the gravity that keeps me grounded. Now that I've found the piece of me that was missing, it feels like home. You're my first thought in the morning, and my last breath at night. I've loved you since you sat next to me in that secluded area of the forest, surrounded by butterflies that didn't even come close to your beauty, and I'll keep loving you until the stars forget to shine."

Valeria's eyes soften, her lips barely brushing mine as she replies, "And I love *you,* Ronnie. I'd been searching for a place to belong, and I found it in your arms. You are the love I've dreamed of, the love I never knew I deserved. I'll follow you anywhere, because with you, I'm not just living—I'm alive," she whispers, pulling me closer.

No matter how close we get, it'll never be enough.

I grin as I stand. "Now, let's get to work. I'm not spending another night without you in my bed."

As she walks past, I slap her ass playfully, and she throws a look over her shoulder. "Do we get to keep the cameras?" she asks, her smirk sultry.

"Yes. Whatever my butterfly wants."

Always.

Acknowledgments

A heartfelt thank you to my readers for taking a chance and exploring something new alongside me! I've always wanted to write FF romance, and when this idea came to light, I knew I had to explore it. I'm so happy I did!

There is a serious shortage of sapphic romances, so I hope this novella motivates readers to consume more sapphic books and writers to come up with new stories!

This novella was brought to life with the help of my amazing alphas— Cláudia, Nikki, Danielle, Jenn, and Naomi! Special shoutout to Cláudia for inspiring this story and translating the Portuguese. Thank you all for taking the time out of your busy schedules to help me polish this story.

All my love!

ALSO BY NOUHA JULLIENNE

Godfathers of the Night Series - Dark Mafia Romance

The Diávolos: Part One

The Diávolos: Part Two

The Sotíras

Sinners and Saints Series - Dark Motorcycle Club Romance

King of Sinners